Seán Dalton & Seán Kelly

Clownbound:
Take Me to the Circuits

www.rwpublishing.net

Clownbound

First published in Ireland in 2018
by Rwpublishing
An RW company

Copyright © Rwpublishing

The right of Seán Dalton and Seán Kelly to be identified as
the authors of the Work has been asserted by them in
accordance with the Copyright and Related Rights Act, 2000.

All rights reserved.
No part of this publication may be reproduced, or transmitted,
in any form without the prior written permission of the
publisher.

All characters in this publication are fictitious and any
resemblance to real persons is coincidental…
ISBN 978-1-9993128-1-7

www.rwpublishing.net

Clownbound

Contents

"If being a clown was easy, everyone would do it..."
-Wongo

Clownbound

Prologue

Welcome to the Clownbound Bookamatic Universe. Before this journey can begin, there are two questions that need to be answered. First, what is the Circus?

Circus

/ 'sar kuuus'/

Noun

 1. A travelling company of acrobats, clowns, and other entertainers which gives performances, typically in a large tent, in a series of different places.

 "I couldn't give a rats whether or not you join the circus. You were a mistake in the first place!"

This is what the internet would have you believe a Circus is. It is understandable that one might see the Circus in this light, but it couldn't be further from the truth. Well, it actually could be further from the truth, but it certainly is not the truth. This story will help shine a light on the true purpose of the Circus.

The second question is even more important. When people think of the Circus they often think of clowns. However, people don't truly understand what a clown is… So, what is a clown?

Clown

/ 'Culown'/

Noun

Clownbound

1.   A comic entertainer, especially one in a Circus, wearing a traditional costume and exaggerated make-up.
"a Circus clown"
Synonyms: comic, entertainer... hero?

<u>A Clown's Limerick</u>

The first clown to exist was named Jay.
"Stop clowning. You'll be taken away!"
He refused to not juggle.
Was led away with a struggle.
Yet clowns have persisted to this day.

03/10/1991 – Yugoslavia

A fogged-up glass in a run-down car, older than the driver himself. A vehicle that was built to fit three managing to fit four. The car was driving down a rural, Yugoslavian road. It wasn't a remarkable car by any means, but it was certainly memorable – It was a three-wheeled three-seater car, painted red with yellow thunder stripes across the sides and made a thumping 'whoop' sound every time the steering wheel was turned. Wedged into the backseat was young little, brittle, Timmy Tim Tim Thompson.

Timmy was a dark haired, shy, young boy with an unfortunate name. His family and friends would often call him 'TT' to save valuable time. Unfortunately, this nickname led to extensive name-calling and bullying in school, with children calling him such names as 'Boobies' and 'Timmy Tit Tit Thompson', because children are oh-so-cruel, and not very creative. In addition to these hurtful words, the life he lived pained him more than any regular boy could fathom. Luckily, Timmy was no regular boy.

Clownbound

Uncommonly for boys living in Yugoslavia, Timmy was born into a drastically poor family with an aggressive father who hit and verbally abused him. He had one sibling, Gabby-Grimley Thompson, who was often referred to as 'GG', because Gabby-Grimley is a ridiculous name. Being the eldest, GG took the brunt of the beating from their father. So much so, that their father was usually too tired to cause much damage to Timmy, hitting him with mere pillow punches. Everyday followed the same routine for both Timmy and Gabby: breakfast, school, a severe beating, dance lessons, dinner and bed. Unlike most days, however, this day had a light at the end of the tunnel. This day would mark the first holiday of Timmy's life. That's because today Timmy, Gabby, their mother, Lucinda Grimley, and their father, Roger Thompson (AKA 'Thompson'), were going to see the Circus for the first time ever for Lucinda's birthday.

Squashed into the back of the three-seater car, Timmy and Gabby were fighting for inches of space. Gabby would always win, because, despite only being 12 years old, she was an absolute monster. She had arms as big as legs and legs as sturdy as cement blocks, taking after her bear of a father. Timmy was less genetically fortunate, with only his boring brown eyes resembling his fathers. The scrambling and fighting in the backseat made it very difficult for their father to navigate the road. This, combined with the icy, snowy conditions, led to a slippery road trip. Luckily, traffic wasn't a huge issue in Yugoslavia, because, as we all know, rollerblading was the main trend in those times. The car spun out of control several times on the journey, rear ending a number of rollerblade enthusiasts, but they were finally one turn away from the Circus. Timmy's eyes caught a glimpse of the promotional sign for the Circus. It showed Yugoslavia's very own clown, 'Sergeant Slippy', holding a red balloon with the words 'See me live at the next right!' written on it.

'Oh my god, we're almost there!' thought Timmy. He had no idea what to expect. He had never been to a Circus, nor had he ever even seen one on the T.V. However, he had a feeling he was going to enjoy it. He wasn't sure why, but something inside him said, *'You're going to enjoy this.'*

When they finally arrived in the carpark the family emptied out of the car, falling into the snow and gasping for air. As they all stretched their limbs, they caught a glimpse of the Circus activity surrounding them: cotton candy vendors, hotdog stands, and the trumpets of elephants coming from behind the enormous multi-coloured tent that stood before them. This could only be enjoyed for a moment before their father pulled them all into a small group huddle. This huddle was not to hype them up or to play Chinese Whispers, but instead to pass a flask to Gabby and Timmy so they could sneak some alcohol into the event for their father. He had a bad history with clowns and intended to be out of his mind drunk for the entire show.

The family got into position as they made their way towards the entrance. They walked in a straight line with their hands behind their backs, trying their best to hide the smuggled flasks. This suspicious activity caught the attention of the bodyguard, CurlyWurly. CurlyWurly, a doctor turned clown, was given his clown name because of his excellent freekick taking for the Clown Soccer Team 'Silly Billies FC' (FC obviously standing for 'Footballing Clowns'). He had the potential to win Clown Cup gold but had to retire from the sport due to time constraints. Even as a clown he found it hard to juggle his work, family and football into his life. After abandoning his football team, he took up a job as bodyguard for the local Circus. He had to remain on high alert, because he was paid on commission and, if people didn't pay, how would he find the money to send his two children, 'Wibbly' and 'Wobbly' to Clown College?

When taking freekicks, one of the ways that CurlyWurly would always fool the goalkeeper was with his swirly eyes. He used the same technique in his job as a security guard. He would flick his eyes outward, extending his vision, allowing him to keep a close eye on each of the children that might try to sneak in behind him. Thompson noticed that the security guard's technique was flawless. He knew getting in would prove to be trickier than he first anticipated. However, simultaneously he was thinking, *'Ha ha ha! That clown is doing a cross-eyed face! God, I hate them... But I sure do hope there's more of that when we get into the show!'*
Putting his resentment for clowns aside, Thompson knew he had to get CurlyWurly's attention. In an attempt to distract CurlyWurly, Thompson put his arm around him, bringing the clown into a playful headlock. He was pretending to be more drunk than he was and began shouting in a slurred, over-exaggerated Soviet accent, "Ha ha ha, very good, clownman, very good. You are funny, no? Ha ha ha. I will see you in show, yes? Very good, clownman!" The ruse worked like a charm as Lucinda and Gabby snuck in behind the distracted clown.

Timmy and Thompson remained outside with four Circus tickets in hand. They needed to make a quick buck and had a plan up their sleeves. Strangely enough this plan didn't involve selling the spare tickets. Not because there was anything wrong with that plan, but because it hadn't yet crossed their minds. Instead, the task that lay in front of them had been rehearsed for weeks on end. Timmy had to wear fingerless gloves and pretend to be homeless. His father knew he needed to look authentically homeless, so he roughed him up, dislocating his shoulder and laying him down in the snow. He then covered him in snow, to assure he was truly shivering. Thompson then ran behind their car and waited for people to give Timmy money. However, nobody handed him any money. They instead flung money at him and spat in his direction. One man approached Timmy with the rage of a thousand rhinos and threw a coin, barely missing Timmy's face. When he noticed that he missed, he went over, picked up the coin and threw it at him again – this time nailing him in the forehead. When the money bounced off Timmy's face, he had no choice but to stretch his arm down into the cold white earth and pull out his earnings. Once Thompson was pleased with the amount of money earned, he lifted poor Timmy over his shoulder and laughed, "Quite the businessman you are Timmy, ha ha!" Quite the businessman he was indeed. He laid across his father's shoulder, eyes closed and clenching his coat, while his father tried to get a refund for the two remaining tickets.

"I would like a refund for these two tickets!" said Thompson.

"No refunds, sorry," replied Curlywurly.

"What? Listen here, clown. I want a refund and if you don't give it to me, I can't be blamed for what I do to you!"

"Read the ticket. It clearly says, 'no refunds.'"

"First of all, it's not very 'clear'. It's not very well designed at all. Secondly, if I don't get this refund I'll snap. I swear to God I WILL sue you."

"Sir, please go inside before I call the Clown Cops."

"The 'Clown Cops'? Pftth!"

"Yes sir, the Clown Cops."

"You'll be calling the Clown Morgue when I'm done with you!"

"Sir, there is no such thing as a 'Clown Morgue.' Now please enter the tent and take your seat."

"Why I oughta!" Thompson shook his closed fist in anger as he walked toward the tent.

"Uggggghhhh. I didn't even do anything wrong!" he grumbled under his breath before heading into the Circus.

The tent's interior was gargantuan, seating over 10,000 lucky people. The red stage curved around the edge of the tent, with a lone opera singer standing on top. Timmy and Thompson arrived at their seats just as the Circus was about to begin. They may have been an hour and a half late, but luckily for them the Yugoslavian national anthem is an hour and twenty-four minutes long. Following the anthem, a man rose from below to the center of the stage.

"Herro, everybody!" announced what appeared to be the host for the night. This crude attempt at a stereotypical Chinese accent left a sour taste in the mouths of everyone in the audience.

"Get off the stage, you bigot!" shouted a number of audience members, solidifying the strong anti-racism attitude that Yugoslavians are so famous for.

Suddenly a clown named 'Bam Bam Barnacles' ran to the center of the stage. He was dressed in a suit made out of barnacles and had boxing gloves on. He motioned the audience to clap to a particular rhythm, despite the fact that he couldn't clap due to the gloves. Dumbfounded by what was happening, the audience began to clap and within a minute their claps synched up, creating a roar of rhythm. With that, Bam Bam Barnacles began to chant, "No to racism, no to racism, no to racism." It wasn't long before the whole tent was filled with this chant. Suddenly another clown appeared on stage. The chanting stopped as gasps filled the arena. It was Pedro Pie Thrower, Spain's third highest ranked clown according to the International Clown Ranking Institution. The silence led to tension. This tension led to disbelief as Pedro Pie Thrower landed a pie cleanly on the original hosts face. "Take that Ku Klux Klown!" shouted Pedro. This was met with an 'ooof' and a 'jaysus' from the crowd.

"This racist scandal was merely a gag; a way of engaging the crowd and getting the show under way," said Timmy with absolute astonishment.

"Well obviously, you little retard," quipped Thompson.

Twelve minutes later when the applause died down, another man took to the stage. This man was no clown, yet he did have funny looking attributes. He didn't have a big red nose, but he did have an amusingly small one. He slowly raised his hands and said, "Hello everybody!" in a perfectly Yugoslavian accent. The crowd sighed in relief. A few even cheered and applauded. One audience member shouted, "stay on the stage!" as a callback to the crowds' previous reaction. This was met with some half laughs, a few people muttering "that's not particularly funny," and one person shouting, "Kill yourself!" which prompted a respectable number of laughs.

The funny looking man introduced the first act; a clown named 'Tall Clown', a fitting name. Towering over the funny looking man he began to juggle three rather large indigo-coloured balls. Having never attended a circus before, Timmy found this to be fascinating. He was struggling to comprehend this clown's incredible balance. For the next hour of the show all he could think about were Tall Clown's big blue balls. The second and third act were nothing out of the ordinary for a circus, but Timmy was having a whale of a time. The fourth act sealed the deal for him, as it should have done for any sane person. The curtain rolled up and beneath it was the most fantastical thing a man or woman could ever hope to see. It was a monkey on a unicycle. What a sight. There were no strings here. No mirror tricks. No CGI. This was literally a monkey that was capable of riding a unicycle. *'Not possible!'* is what half of the audience thought. The other half were too caught up with the fact that a monkey was riding a unicycle and couldn't even process a thought. Timmy was thinking about one day meeting that monkey and shaking his hand.

As the fifth act came out this thought process was brought to a halt. Timmy couldn't believe his eyes. His heart dropped as butterflies attacked his stomach. He suddenly felt more vulnerable than ever. The young Yugoslavian had just gotten his first crush on a girl. The girl was slightly older than Timmy, a clown and performed in the trapeze act. With shamrock green eyes sparkling like an animal balloon in the sunlight, Timmy couldn't lose eye contact. She was the first of her kind. A new breed of Circus Act performing in multiple aspects of the circus. Her parents called her Hybrid. They named her this, because they had dreamed of their daughter becoming a two-act prodigy in the circus. This led to serious bullying and name-calling like 'fatso' and 'yellow belly', but her parents didn't care. All they cared about was the circus buzz.

As she went to perform in front of 10,000 strangers, she locked eyes with Timmy. What happened next was a rare occurrence. True love. Timmy's jaw dropped as he felt their souls intertwine, and it was clear from her expression that she was experiencing the same thrill. This moment of beauty felt like an eternity for both of them. For him, it was as though her love had pierced his soul creating a hole only to be filled by her affection. For her, it felt like she had known Timmy her whole life, as though she knew him better than she knew herself. Within that short moment their eyes would be truly opened forever. They suddenly understood William Shakespeare's love poems and Gustav Klimt's painting 'The

Kiss'. Life suddenly made sense. As their eyes parted Timmy became a new person. His whole perspective had shifted. He stopped thinking about big blue balls and began wondering about what he was going to say to Hybrid. She went on to perform with such elegance and grace. Everybody in the audience was enthralled by her skill. She trapezed left and she trapezed right. She even did a 360 degrees trapeze which was met with thunderous applause.

Once the show was over Timmy nervously made his way over to Hybrid. She was sitting on her own with her arms crossed by her chest. She looked up and when she saw Timmy's face she smiled and put her arms down by her side.

"Hey. I saw you in the show. You were really good." Timmy's voice was shaky.

"Hey! Thank you! I saw you in the audience, believe it or not."

"I doubt that," said Timmy with diffidence. "There were thousands of us there. And loads of super good looking, purebred Yugoslavians. I'm no match for them."

"Well it wasn't their eyes I caught…" said Hybrid with a smile. "Let me just get this clown makeup off."

"No. Keep it on."

"Oh… Okay."

"I think you're gorgeous even with all that makeup on. You don't need a clean face to be beautiful."

"Aww thank you!" Hybrid started to blush. "What are you doing tonight?"

"Well I've dance lessons in an hour, but other than that nothing really. Why?"

"We could meet up at the tent later tonight and I could show you around. If you want to."

"I'd love to! After my dance lessons of course."

"Of course. Okay, how does 7pm sound?"

"Oooof dancing starts at 6:30pm."

"What about 7:30pm then?"

Timmy started counting on his fingers. "Ehhh, 9?"

"9 what?"

Timmy started counting on his fingers again. "9pm."

"Ohh! Yeah 9pm works for me!"

"Cool! I can't wait!"

Timmy made his way back to the car where his parents snapped at him for taking so long. As a result, he had to spend the journey home in the trunk of the car with only his wandering mind and three bowling balls. Lying in the trunk with a big smile on his face, Timmy could not wait to meet up with Hybrid later that night. Little did Timmy know that this night was the night his life was going to change forever.

2: The Circus Giveth and Taketh Away

Timmy told his mother and father that he had a big date with a girl he had recently met. To his surprise, they actually seemed to be happy for him.

"Way to go!" said his mother.

"Great! Hopefully you can move in with her and get the fuck out of my house," said his father.

Timmy wore grey trousers, a crisp white shirt and a black, woollen V-neck jumper. He slicked his hair back with gel. He was dressed to impress. Thompson, however, was unimpressed.

"Son, this is your first date. She must swoon. You need to make her heart melt the moment she sees you!" said Thompson as he shook his head. "This simply will not do. Try these instead." He handed him one of his old tuxedos and a pair of laced black shoes. Timmy took the clothes into the bathroom and quickly changed. Wearing waist size 38 trousers and a white shirt with a chest size of 25 inches, Timmy looked absolutely ridiculous. His hands were met by the inside elbow of the shirt. The shoes were far too big for him, making him look like a clown. *'This might just work,'* thought Timmy. He walked back out to his parents, who gave mixed reactions.

"Wow… You look almost as good as me in that, Timmy," said Thompson.

"You look ridiculous, Timmy. I don't mean that as a joke. If I were her and I saw you like that, I would run away," said his mother.

"Don't mind her, Timmy! She doesn't know fashion like your old man! Anyway, where is this big date?"

"Oh I'm just taking her to the movies…" lied Timmy. He didn't want his parents to know he was going back to the Circus because he knew that his father hates clowns. The last thing he wanted to do was anger him.

"Just make sure you're home by 12!" shouted his mother as he left out the back door.

Once he was in the garden he had to make his way back to the Circus tent. Luckily, the Circus was located directly beside their house. There was only a wall between the Circus and their house. Because of this, and because they wanted to bring the car, they had to drive 20 minutes to get there earlier in the day. Timmy approached the wall and climbed over it like a man that needed to get over a wall. Once over, his feet felt the cobblestone ground leading into the makeshift tent. It was exactly like it was earlier except now there were no parked cars, no security guards, and everything was completely different. He felt the brisk Yugoslavian wind blow through his gelled back hair as he walked towards the tent. Standing outside the tent, wearing loose polka dotted trousers and a hilariously oversized white shirt, was Hybrid.

She was wearing the same clothes from when she had seen Timmy earlier. In that moment Timmy froze. He started to breathe heavily. Not from the poor air quality or fatigue, not from lack of lung capacity; from fear. Genuine fear. He had yet to take time to reflect on what was about to happen… His first date. The nerves suddenly hit him like a frisbee to the face of a blind man. He approached her with his palms sweating, his neck stiffened. Timmy looked down to avoid eye contact as he sheepishly walked towards her. He looked up. He gazed into her green eyes, and noticed her cheeks were blushing. Within a moment of looking into her eyes, he calmed down. He felt relaxed and natural.

"Hey!" said Timmy.

"Hey… How are you?" replied Hybrid.

"Good… I mean, great! What about you?"

"Great as well!" There was suddenly a silence.

Timmy thought back to what his father told him about women: "Just ask them questions, they LOVE talking about themselves!"

"You're very good at that trapezing stuff," said Timmy. "Where'd you learn that?"

"I was sent to a trapeze boarding school for 2 years. Then I did a 3-year stint at a clown boarding school. Parents orders."

"Damn. That's crazy."

"'Crazy' is one word for it."

"Do you not like it?"

"I do. It's just… I don't know…" Hybrid hesitated.

"Is this not what you want to be doing?"

"Nah, it is. I'm a clown through and through. It's just… I'm not in love with trapezing, you know? I just want to be a clown, but they keep putting me on as the trapeze act. It sucks."

"What could possibly be so great about being a clown?"

"Are you making fun of my craft?"

"Maybe."

"Well, are you enjoying doing that?"

"Hell yeah!"

"So, you're saying you enjoy *clowning* on my dreams?"

"Yeah."

"So, you admit clowning is enjoyable?" she said with a smirk as she folded her arms.

"Ha ha alright… Alright! You got me! Sorry for questioning you."

"Don't be sorry!" said Hybrid. She gazed into Timmy's eyes with fascination. "Have you ever thought about becoming a clown?"

"Me?" Timmy shook his head. "I wouldn't have it in me. Plus, my parents would never let me. My father hates clowns."

Just as Hybrid was about to interject, they heard a noise from inside the tent.

"What was that?" asked Timmy.

"I'm not sure. Let's go in and find out!"

They walked in only to find a clown screaming at the top of their lungs.

"What's going on?" asked Hybrid.

The clown turned around. "I saw a spider." The clown leaned in with a cheesy smirk slipping out. "I was so scared, I almost WEB myself!" The clown erupted into laughter and tumbled away.

"Ugh, he makes that joke every week. It's not even a good joke," said Hybrid. Timmy nodded in agreement, while thinking *'Ha ha ha not bad... not bad!'*

"Anyway," said Hybrid, "we might as well go inside."

They walked around the huge tent as Timmy followed Hybrid around.

"Tell me," started Timmy, "how did they keep the monkey on the unicycle, because I know there's no chance that he stayed on that himself!

"He's a she. And yes, she did."

"That's incredible!"

"Not really. It's a unicycle, almost everybody in the Circus knows how to ride one."

"But she's a monkey."

"So?"

Clownbound

"I'm so confused. How can a monkey ride a unicycle and why is it not a big deal? I feel like it should be a big deal."

"They train. Like anybody else. What you saw was her riding the unicycle. What you didn't see was the many failed attempts before that and the 50 dead monkeys that preceded her."

"I guess so."

"So," said Hybrid, trying to shift the conversation, "would you like me to show you around?"

"I'd love that!"

Hybrid put out her hand for Timmy to grab. Timmy couldn't believe it. This was the first time he'd ever held a girl's hand – excluding Gabby's hands of steel. He put his hand on hers and followed her lead. She brought him to the bottom of the tent. She showed him what goes on in the background of the Circus; things that, if made public, would cause outcry. She showed him how they force the seal to balance a ball on his head despite knowing that the seal has vertigo. She let him meet the elephants that were held hostage backstage, despite not being used in the show. She revealed that the cotton candy contained barley, even though they were clearly marketing it as 'Gluten Free'. Not everything was bad, however. She also showed him some of the amazing things in the Circus; the local Clown Priest offering confession to all of the Christian Clowns (15% of all clowns), the recycling clowns separating plastics and cardboard from that evenings show, and a small organisation of clowns set up to prevent and eradicate childhood obesity in Yugoslavia. Timmy was amazed at how complex Circus life truly was. They continued walking around the front of the tent.

"What's in there?"

"There?" said Hybrid as she pointed at a mahogany door just left of where they were standing. "Oh Timmy, that's the freakshow room. That's where all the freaks stay."

"Freaks?"

"Yeah, the freaks."

"Who are 'the freaks'?"

"The most annoying people you'll ever meet, Timmy. Be happy you don't know them. They're the really tall men who *aren't* using stilts. The people with 3 or 6 fingers. The women with beards. The mermaids. The snail man—"

"What? Mermaids? Snail man? Who's the snail man?"

"Yes, mermaids. And he's the man who looks like a snail."

"As in his face looks like a snail?"

"No, his whole body does. He looks exactly like a snail, except he's human size."

"What! That's crazy!"

"Yeah, I know. It's so strange."

"Can I see him?"

Hybrid thought about this for a moment. "No."

"Oh, okay…"

They continued walking and walked past a slightly opened carmine coloured door. Timmy peered through the gap in the door. Two lions lay on top of some man, purring and licking their arms.

"Ehhh, are they the lions from the show?"

"Oh, you weren't supposed to see that…" said Hybrid. "Yeah, the lion tamers have truly tamed these lions."

"So, they're lying to the audience?"

"I think you mean they're LION to the audience!" laughed Hybrid. When both she and Timmy stopped rolling over with laughter she continued, "To be fair, nobody wants to see a bunch of big cats licking themselves on stage."

Clownbound

"I'm sorry to say, but there are so many people that would LOVE to see that, myself included. That's why zoos are so popular. But, I can kind of see what you mean."

They sat down on a bench near the end of the tent. Timmy was nervously planning how he was going to try kiss Hybrid in his head. He knew he had to seal the deal. He hadn't been at the Circus for too long, but he saw the other men around and knew his competition would be as stiff as the nails used to pin down the Circus tent.

"I hope I'm not boring you with all this Circus stuff…" said Hybrid.

"Are you kidding me? This has been an amazing night. I didn't realise how much I liked the Circus."

"You should join."

"Who? Me? I couldn't…"

"Why not?"

"I just… I don't think I have it in me, you know?"

Hybrid gazed directly into Timmy's eyes. "I know a clown when I see one and goddammit Timmy, you're a clown! I can see it in your eyes. It's inside you! There's no avoiding this. You can't hide from yourself!"

Timmy felt a rush of adrenaline and leaned in to kiss Hybrid. Suddenly, he pulled back.   "Oh shit, here comes my mother!" cried Timmy. "What the hell, she said I could stay out until 12 o'clock and it's only 11 o'clock!"

"Wait, look," said Hybrid as she pointed towards Timmy's mother. She walked right past them, without even glancing an eye in their direction. She walked into a room near the end of the tent. "That's Wongo's office…"

"Who's Wongo?"

"The infamous Wongo! The clown that bought all the drugs in the world so that no children could ever buy drugs again!"

"Wow! And that worked?"

"No. No, not at all. In fact, he just ended up funding the drug cartels, allowing them to produce more drugs than ever before. Child drug use levels flew through the roof. However, he had good intent. He meant well."

"Oh, that's unfortunate."

"Yeah, it is. He's also the leader of this branch of the Circus. Why is your mother going in there?"

Timmy didn't respond. He just sat there, confused and uneasy as he stared at the door to Wongo's office. Suddenly, ten clowns swung the door open and marched into the office. The next thing Timmy saw was the ten clowns dragging his mother away. He ran towards them and helplessly watched as the clowns stuffed his mother into an extremely small car that only went up to her knee, before all ten hopped in after her. As soon as they were all wedged in, one of the clowns leaned out of the car, slapped the roof, put two fingers in his mouth and whistled. With that, the Clown Car hit 100km/h in about three seconds and shot down the road.

<u>A Trapeze Artist's Rap</u>

Bar hanging from the ceiling (yuh yuh)
Y'already know

Am I gonna hang from it? (Skrt skrt)
I sure think so

When we perform (whaaat)
Ya'll get chills (yuh)

Got mad stability (huh?)
Like we on balance pills (yeah)

"Holy mackerel Hybrid, that was my mother!" Timmy said, squeezing her hand much tighter than before. "What was my mother doing here? What did Wongo do to her? How did so many people fit into such a small car?"

"Okay Okay Timmy, calm down," said Hybrid. "Wongo is a reasonable clown. He has a heart of gold! I'm sure whatever the problem is, he can straighten it out as well as he straightens out balloons before he ties them up into animals."

The infatuated pair walked over to Wongo's office. Outside the entrance they could still smell the burning petrol from the Clown Car's harsh revs when it left. The tiny tyre tracks were fresh from the two totally sick donuts it made before it sped off. Hybrid knocked on Wongo's door in the rhythm of her signature knock, to identify herself. Her signature knock was to the beat of 'The Clownbound Theme Song'.

Clownbound

Through the hallow, white painted wooden door, Wongo could be vaguely heard saying, "Ah that'll be JimJams," before letting out a roar, "C'mon in!"

Hybrid twisted the red door knob. The red knob was a 3-D replica of a clown's nose. She then glided the door open to let herself in with Timmy following, hidden behind her. Wongo had his back facing the pair and seemed to be reading a comically oversized book, something called a new-s-pa-per. More than likely just another one of those silly clown habits.

"Ah, JimJams, you're right on time for tickle pract—" Wongo turned around and saw who his guests really were. "You're not JimJams." Timmy then walked in further to stand side by side with Hybrid. "You're not JimJams either. I can't fucking believe JimJams is late again."

"Sir, it's me, Hybrid."

"Well Hybrid, what's your knock rhythm?"

"The Clownbound Theme Song."

"Well it shouldn't be. That's JimJams' knock."

"I don't know what to tell you Wongo, but it's mine as well. It might be something that needs to be sorted out."

"Suppose so. Anyways Hybrid, how can I help you and your fri-… Timmy. Hello, Timmy. Nevermind. I know why you're here."

Bewildered by the fact that the clown knew his name, Timmy took a step back. His heart sank, and he suddenly became flustered, struggling for air. "How do you know my name?"

"Oh Timmy, Timmy, Timmy. We have much to tell you. You might want to take a seat." Wongo proceeded to grab two of Bam Bam Barnacle's stools from the corner of his office, which were made of barnacles. He then set it up for Timmy and Hybrid on the other side of his desk. Timmy and Hybrid sat down. Hybrid spoke up, thinking this would be a hard situation for Timmy.

"Wongo, we saw what happened outside and—"

"P-p-please tell me what you're doing with her," interrupted Timmy, fearing for his mother's well-being.

The clown chuckled and said, "Where to begin... You see, Timmy, your mother is not who you think she is. Oh no, in fact quite the contrary. She is who you don't think she is. She has been misleading you and your family for years." Wongo took a drink through his unnecessarily long crazy straw resting on the desk in front of him. "In fact, she is not your real mother at all, nor is she even from Yugoslavia."

"What are you even talking about?" interjected Timmy. "This is ridiculous, even by a clown's standards."

"Timmy, have you never questioned why your parents speak English all the time? Have you never wondered why they talk with American accents?" Wongo questioned, drawing on his eyebrows higher with a paint brush he pulled out from his desk drawer.

"Well I always assumed it was because the Eastern European accent won't get you a job, but no I never really thought about it..." Timmy looked down at the ground. He began to question everything in his head.

"I think you're going to want to see this, Timmy." The clown then honked his nose, spun his Dicky bow and said, "Follow me."

As Timmy leapt from his stool the clown made his way around the desk to the couple and extended his hands for both of them to grab. They both put their hands on Wongo's simultaneously, and as they did, they both felt a shock race through their bodies to the point where they had to let go of the clown's hand. Timmy was puzzled by what just happened. Hybrid was disappointed for falling for that trick again.

"HAH gotcha," laughed Wongo, as he revealed an electric buzzer in each hand.

'Genius,' thought Timmy as he followed the clown through a slide door disguised as a wall behind the desk. Wongo looked back and saw Hybrid still in his office.

"Are you not coming?"

"No, it's okay. I'll see you tomorrow, Timmy. This seems like it's for your eyes only."

Timmy turned back, gave Hybrid a hug, and whispered, "Tomorrow's going to be a great day then."

They closed their eyes and the moment lasted longer than they both expected, until they heard a knock that resembled the rhythm of the 'The Clownbound Theme Song.' Wongo barged by the hugging couple and knocked them both over. He then pulled open the door and, seeing who it was, he began to scream.

"JIMJAMS YOU ARE LATE FOR THE LAST TIME! I'VE GIVEN YOU COUNTLESS SECOND CHANCES AND YOU STILL HAVE THE NERVE TO WASTE MY TIME."

During this time all Timmy and Hybrid could hear, other than Wongo screaming, were aggressive monkey shouts and taunts from the other side of the door.

"NOW YOU CAN TAKE YOUR UNICYCLE AND FUCK OFF BACK TO THE BANANA ROOM!" Wongo slammed the door and straightened out his dyed red hair in an attempt to act casual again. "Now, are you ready, Timmy?" he said in a deeper, more stressed voice than before.

Wongo and Timmy then left the room and headed towards the basement of the tent. Computers and hard drives filled the room that they had walked into, nothing like Timmy could ever have even dreamed of. The room was purely lit by flicking red lights and huge monitor screens.

"What is this place?" questioned Timmy, looking around the room in shock.

"Timmy... what is it you think we clowns do?"

"You entertain the people?"

"HA HA no, my son... we protect the people!" said the clown with a proud look on his face, hidden behind the surprised look of the makeup.

"Well that's ridiculous."

Wongo laughed and hit Timmy with a checkmate comeback, "Ridiculously true!"

Timmy shook his head. "I must be dreaming. This doesn't make any sense. I need to sit down."

Wongo grabbed one of the lions' stools and handed it to Timmy. "Look Timmy, this is difficult to explain. To make a long story short, your mother was involved with a very dangerous group of Bandit Clowns. These are clowns that have gone rogue and who work for the highest bidder. We are not sure why she married your father, but it wasn't for love... there was an alternative reason... We do know, however, that she was planning on assassinating me tonight. That's why she showed up, to try put an end to me. Thankfully, I'm a blue belt in Karate. She didn't knock, but I heard the door open. 'INTRUDER!' I thought. So, I ran up to her and kicked her as hard as I could in the shin. This gave security plenty of time to answer my calls for help, so I was able to defend myself until they came in."

"What!? that's absolutely insane... So, the Rogue Clowns wanted you dead?" said Timmy with genuine interest.

"Jesus Christ Timmy, obviously not." Wongo stopped, let out a sigh and rolled his eyes. "No, these Bandit Clowns don't care if I'm dead or alive. It makes no difference to them. They just do it for the money. That's all they care about. They'll work for anybody."

"Anybody?"

"*Anybody*," said Wongo with a wink.

Timmy leaned in and asked, "Then who wanted you dead?"

"You might be a bit too young to know this, but the Magicians have wanted me dead for years. Being the number one clown in the world puts a big bullseye on my back and the Magicians have been throwing darts for years. They're trying to start another war within the Circus."

"'Another' war!?"

"Calm down you lunatic, you'll wake the computers. They're sleeping."

"Oh sorry."

"But yes, there is another war brewing. A war bigger than any war you could ever imagine. A war between the Clowns and the Magicians!"

"My God."

"And this could get out of hand fast. If your 'mother' had been successful tonight, all hell would have broken loose. Luckily, she wasn't. But it was a close call."

"But I don't understand. Why did she marry my father? Why was she pretending to be my mother? What did that have to do with assassinating you?"

"Unfortunately, we do not know… We can only assume they're completely unrelated. However, as I already said, she was married to your father for a reason. We just don't know the reason. We now know she was paid to assassinate me and had been plotting the assassination for two years."

They walked into the back office of the computer room, which looked like an exact replica of Wongo's normal office. Here Timmy was greeted by Lieutenant Loose Eyes, a clown whose eyes were truly out of place.

"Is this the boy?" asked Loose Eyes.

"Yes, this is Timmy Tim Tim Thompson."

"Have you told him about his real mother yet?"

Timmy interrupted both clowns and said, "My real mother? You know her? This is crazy!"

"Goddammit Loose Eyes the kid isn't ready for that story yet. Have you gone mad! Sorry Timmy, we can't tell you about that today."

"No, no that's not fair. You have to tell me!" shouted Timmy.

"Sorry Timmy but he's right," admitted Loose Eyes.

Timmy interrupted again saying "No, tell me please!"

"Here Timmy, shut the fuck up for a second. You're doing our heads in. Stop asking questions," said Wongo with clear frustration. "We're trying to figure out what we're going to do with you and your sibling."

"Sibling?" asked Lieutenant Loose Eyes as his eyes wandered.

"Yes, his half-sister!" Loose Eyes wrote something down on his notepad.

Timmy's face dropped. "Please don't kill us," cried Timmy.

Both clowns erupted into laughter. "HA HA! Timmy we're not going to hurt you, don't worry. We just need to find you a new family," said Loose Eyes, trying to wipe the tears of laughter from his crazy eyes.

"Let me join the circus! I now feel like this is what I'm destined to do. Even Hybrid said I'd be great! Let me join please," pleaded Timmy.

"Are you out of your damn mind, Timmy?" shouted Wongo. "We can't just let you join the circus! You don't even have a Clown Diploma, let alone your Crazy Clown Certificate. We can't just let every kid whose mother's an undercover Clown Bandit and whose father's a drunk join the circus."

Timmy stood his ground. "I am going to Clown College! I'm doing it for Hybrid. If she thinks I can do it, then I can do it! She looked me in the eyes and said she saw a clown in me... I swear she meant it! At least figuratively anyway. She wasn't just saying it!"

Wongo turned his back to Timmy and then turned back around to face Timmy. Wongo had drawn a very detailed, profound look on his face with his paint brush, while he thought about Timmy's choice. "You know what, Timmy? You do that! If she thinks you can do it, then so do I! But make no mistake about it, Timmy... Clown College is not easy. If it were easy, everybody would be a clown. You are going to have to work harder than you've ever worked, and even then, that might not be enough. You'll have to sacrifice everything. Your health. Your friendships. Any hobbies you may have. All of it. Can you do that, Timmy? Are you capable of being a clown?"

Timmy stood up. He straightened his back and began walking around the room, asserting his dominance. The two clowns were taken aback. They looked on with amazement. He stood between the two men, pointing his index finger at both of them, back and forth, before stopping. The room went silent. Timmy pointed to himself and bellowed his voice across the whole tent.

"I'm not just going to be a clown. I'm going to be the best damn clown the world has ever seen!" and with that he stormed out of the room, slamming the slide door behind him leaving a sense of pride and wonder in the computer room.

"His real mother would be proud," said Loose Eyes as he turned his deranged eyes towards Wongo.

4: A Romantic Montage

Over the next few years Timmy and Hybrid grew closer and closer. Their relationship blossomed into something special. The two were inseparable and became somewhat dependent on each other, struggling to go a day without seeing one another. Timmy, a boy who was frail, shy and weak, was suddenly as confident as a cat that had just chased a bear up a tree. Hybrid brought out the best in him, turning him from a boy to a man. As well as this, Timmy began hitting the gym. With his father's genetics, he started to see results very quickly. His calves looked as though they were carved by the Greek Gods. His glutes looked as though he stuffed them with finely cut steel. His chest and shoulders appeared to have doubled in size. All of a sudden, he started to earn a lot more respect from people he didn't even know. Men would come up to him and ask, "How do you do it?" Women would approach him and ask for his number, but he'd always decline, saying, "Sorry ladies, this hot piece of ass is taken!"

During these loved-up years, Timmy and Hybrid went on over one hundred dates. These included mini-golf, zorbing, seven minutes in heaven and several dance contests (which Timmy won every time). They also had their ups and downs. When Timmy first began accumulating mass, he was unaware of just how strong he was getting. This led to him accidently throwing Hybrid through the ceiling when they were rehearsing for a break-dancing competition. Hybrid wasn't too happy about this. They didn't speak for the next week, mainly because she was in hospital and wasn't allowed visitors for a week. When he was allowed visit, Timmy showed up with

Hybrid's favourite flowers and chocolates; Roses and Roses. They soon made up and Timmy learned to control his newfound strength. A few months into the relationship Hybrid commented on Timmy's dancing, saying, "Your right leg was a bit stiff for the second part of the dance…"

Timmy refused to even look at Hybrid for several weeks. He was genuinely distraught and didn't leave his bed for days. Eventually, Hybrid showed up at Timmy's school and apologised. She brought a stereo and held it over her head, blaring '*I Wanna Dance with Somebody*' by Whitney Houston. He accepted the apology but still thinks about the comment every night. Other than these two incidents their relationship was smooth sailing. They were truly in love.

Once she turned 18, Hybrid flew to Switzerland to attend the prestigious Clown College of Zurich. She was disappointed that she wouldn't see Timmy for a while, but she had wanted to earn her 'Crazy Clown Certificate' for years and that time had finally come. She packed her bags and left, leaving Timmy temporarily heartbroken. He spent weeks reading books called; 'How to make long-distance relationships work' and 'How to maintain my long-distance relationship with my clown girlfriend while she's in Clown College'. These books slightly helped Timmy, but he still struggled. He agreed that he was going to attend the same university once he finished high school, however he was still awaiting his acceptance letter.

All in all, Hybrid became a crutch for Timmy. He envisioned a future with her, multiple children and a dog named Clive. He knew that he would treat his children right and learn from his parent's mistakes. He wanted his children to live the lives they wanted. He wasn't going to force them into Clownhood, but then again, they would have the divine birth right to do so if they pleased. Everything seemed to be lining up perfectly for him. He was happier than he had ever been, and it was all thanks to his relationship with Hybrid. The last thing Timmy needed was for her to die… Anyway, onto the next chapter.

A Contortionist's Couplet

Into unique positions I can twist and bend,
With other Circus acts I do not blend.

16/12/1995 – Bosnia and Herzegovina

Timmy mightn't have had Hybrid by his side anymore, but he didn't allow that to stray him away from his goal. High school can be a tough time for a kid, but it can be an even tougher time for a clown. Nobody takes you seriously as a clown. However, Timmy took being a clown very seriously. He spent every spare moment of his life practicing being a clown. He wanted to fully prepare for Clown College. Unfortunately, it was getting late in the school year and his acceptance letter still had not arrived.

Timmy excelled in all of his classes in school. He embodied the perfect combination of being a teacher's pet and super-duper cool amongst his classmates. His entire life had taken one big U-turn. He was now living in a one-bedroom apartment in what was now known as Bosnia and Herzegovina. The fall of Yugoslavia left a sour taste in his mouth and the collapse of his family hurt him even more so. He had been separated from Gabby and hadn't seen her in years. He rarely thought of his old so-called family, but when he did, he wept. He would often excuse himself to the bathroom in the middle of the class to figuratively peel some onions. For the fact that Timmy was a rockin' hot shot, not a soul ever suspected that he would be sobbing in them bathrooms. Of course, roars of sadness were often heard coming from the bathroom. These roars were thought to come from 'Domestic Dave'.

Domestic Dave was routinely coming into school with bruises and scars, mostly surrounding his face. Dave was a perfect example of how depression could attack anyone and that nobody's mental health is safe. He was ruggedly handsome with muscles bulging out so far that he would have to shimmy through doors sideways to fit on by. He attended the High School full time on a boarding school basis, only going to visit his parents at home on weekends. Yes, the weekends were truly the weak ends of Dave's life. Because, unfortunately… Dave played for his domestic rugby club and they were constantly in a relegation battle, putting immense pressure on Domestic Dave as captain. Dave regularly got the brunt of the blame for any crying going on in the school, leaving Timmy the freedom to cry away wherever he saw fit and pass the blame onto Dave. This was a shame because Timmy and Dave got on extremely well in school. They were both athletes, so they always had a lot to talk about, whether it was the topic of training or the pressure of certain sporting situations. Timmy promised himself that he would only begin to feel bad about spreading the rumors the day Dave catches him out.

He was one of the top prospects in the slightly below privileged school he was attending. It was considered "slightly below privilege" because nothing about living in Bosnia was a privilege. Cold, depression and grumpy people were the only things that surround you. There were no privileged schools. This was the best one. This was as good as it got. Being in such a position, he was encouraged to not only attend college, but achieve a prestigious degree from college. The counselors and even the principal expected Timmy to become a doctor, or at the very least attend law school. They all sensed lunacy in Timmy's behavior as he was still hellbent on completing Hybrid's vision of becoming a top clown. He felt his chances of becoming a clown were diminishing as he was constantly being pulled out of class for talks about his future. As well as this, he feared that he might potentially become unfunny and boring with all the studying he'd been doing. He could not allow this to happen. To combat this problem, he made funny faces in the mirror for four hours every day.

Timmy thought back to a simpler time; a time when the only people he had to worry about were himself, Hybrid and Wongo. Wongo had set him up with an impressive apartment in the middle of Bosnia.

"Try not to burn it down with all the pies you'll be cooking!" Wongo shouted six years ago. If Timmy closed his eyes and concentrated as hard as he could, he could still hear the echoes from the outrageously hard slapping of Wongo's knee as he went into a laughing fit. **BANG BANG BANG!** Hit with such might that he dislocated his knee cap. Timmy had already walked out the door because he thought the conversation had ended. Little did he know, Wongo literally bled out from his knee after Timmy had left the room. Dying from laughter; the noblest way a clown could possibly leave this world. This death was classed as highly irregular and suspicious as no body was recovered.

The first thing Timmy would do every day after school was practice his dance moves. After this, he would search through his mail in the hopes of finding his acceptance letter. He even formed a friendship with the mailman. Every day when the mailman showed up, he would yell out, "Wazzzzup!", while sticking his tongue out and shaking his head. Keep in mind this was before the film *'Scary Movie'* came out so this was a very unusual thing for someone to do. Nonetheless one day after school Timmy heard a roar of "Wazzzzzup!" and mail came flying through his mailbox. He read the front of each envelope. Letters from the taxman and someone called 'DDD'. He had almost given up hope when at last a long-anticipated envelope from the 'Clown College of Zurich' sat in his hand. Timmy unsealed the big red nose sticker holding down the flap of the envelop. It read:

Well hello there Timmy!

Well gee whiz! We heard over here that you think you're a funny kid! But from your grades we think you're telling a tale as long as my shoes. If you are still interested in learning with us, give us a honk, unless you're just tooting your own horn that is! I'm sure that you are already aware, but we are located on Funny Lane in Clown Village, in Zurich. There is a security dog after you come in the entrance. Just make sure after you knick knack that you give that dog a bone.

As well as this, beware the high school cycle is a lot different to the Unicycle.

Regards,

Professor McClownclown, the Dean of this here university.

Well, by golly, didn't Timmy burst out with excitement. He began to prepare immediately. This was it, the shot he'd been waiting for. He could barely contain the joy he was feeling. The first thing that popped into his mind was 'Hybrid' and how he had to tell her the news straight away. He picked up his letter writing equipment and began to write a short letter to her. He wrote:

Hybrid,

Clownbound

I'm on my way...

6: Adult Lessons From Adolescents

08/10/1996 - Switzerland

Timmy arrived at Clown College on a Saturday afternoon, with his suitcase, a big smile, and a pocket full of ready-made animal balloons. As he walked along the Clown Campus towards his dorm room, he felt like a million bucks. When he got to his room he was met by his roommate, a tall, African American man with glasses named Steve.

"Hey dude, I'm Steve! I just came in from the States this morning. I guess this means we're roommates, huh?"

"Hi, I'm Timmy Tim Tim Thompson, but you can call me Timmy," said Timmy, even though the only thing going through his mind was *'don't say the N word. Don't do it Timmy, don't say it.'*

"Okay Timmy, that's pretty sweet. I can't wait to start throwing pies and clowning around! I've always wanted to be a clown," said Steve with pride.

"Yeah, that'll be good fun," said Timmy, just about avoiding using the 'N word'.

"Anyway Timmy, I got to go meet Professor McClownclown, so I'll see you around!" Steve opened the door to leave.

"Yeah okay, see you!" said Timmy, as he closed the door behind him. Timmy was disgusted that they had put him in the same room as a guy like Steve. He couldn't believe how unlucky he was to have the share a room with the one type of person he despised: people with glasses. Fricking nerds. This was not the start to college life that Timmy had hoped for. Little did he know, it was about to get worse.

From that point on, college life was full speed ahead. Timmy didn't even have time to unpack before his only class of the day started. He needed to leave immediately if he was going to have a chance of being on time. He grabbed a notepad and pen out from his suitcase and dashed out the door, not being totally sure where he had to be. The class he was currently missing was Home-Economics, a subject only taken up by people who were determined to go down the stream of being a world-class clown. Timmy rushed around the campus looking for the Hula Hoop building. He couldn't ask anyone as all the students and teachers around him were already busy trying to make it to their own classes via cartwheels. Eventually, he found a map that showed he wasn't too far away after all. Looking like an absolute amateur running to the hula hoop building, he was still unsure of what room he needed to get to. The building of course, was shaped like a huge hula hoop lying down. He began to circle it hoping to get lucky.

Out of the blue, Timmy was yelled at, "HEY! KID! STOP RIGHT THERE!"

Timmy turned around and saw a clown cartwheel toward him. The halls were empty, so Timmy knew that he was talking to him. When he stopped cartwheeling over to Timmy, he stood up as straight as an arrow. He was wearing an official police uniform and clown makeup with an unorthodox brushy moustache to match it.

"What do you think you're doing, kid?"

"Going to class sir," Timmy said, blushing behind his make-up.

"Boy where do you think you are? This is not acceptable!" The Police Clown said, clearly growing impatient.

"What do you mean sir? It's my first day…what am I doing wrong?"

Clownbound

The Police Clown rolled his eyes. He then pulled a hula hoop half the size of Timmy from one back pocket. Following that, he pulled half a metre-stick from his other back pocket. "When you are in the hula hoop building, you will ACT appropriately. Now use that stick to roll your hula hoop wherever you go in this building. Don't let me catch you dropping the hula hoop either."

"Oh, no problem. Thank you, Sir!"

"Now get the fuck out of my sight or I'll break your legs," said the Police Clown shaking his clown paw.

Timmy was now running through the hallways with a hula hoop rolling in front of him. Moments after he left the Police Clown, he spotted a sign for Home-Economics. Overcome with relief he went to the room. It took him only a few seconds to get there. He lifted his hula hoop and opened the door. The class was about half full and went silent when the door opened. They all initially thought it was the teacher. Timmy closed the door after him, and the class resumed talking with each other. After closing the door, he realized there was a hula hoop hook on the back of the door. He stuck his up there with the others and brought the stick with him down to a chair at the front, where nobody else was sitting. If he wanted to be top of this class, he knew he would have to be sitting here all year.

Another five minutes had passed, and the class was still lecturer-less. Timmy was starting to feel stupid for rushing himself to get to this class. Then there she was, the class lecturer. It was hard to determine whether it was a he or a she, but their voice was quite feminine. Everyone sat up straight and gazed up to the top of the room. This was the beginning of the rest of their lives. The lecturer immediately sensed this serious atmosphere and was sick of it already. To break the mood, she moonwalked her way to her desk which was met by astonished faces, followed by 'oooohs' and 'aaahhhs' from the students. (Not the moonwalk the dance, but the actual way they walked on the moon. Very slowly.)

"Houston, we have a problem," she said in a Darth Vader kind of voice.

"What's the problem Ms. Astronaut?" she said, replying to herself.

"We've got a room of dead serious clowns!" she said, bursting into laughter but leaving the classroom cringing.

Wiping away a tear of laughter she continued, "I'm not really 'Ms. Astronaut' I'm actually Mrs. Bobbles and sorry I'm late! I was at the newly opened Clown Morgue identifying 16 Clown Orphans and the two owners of the Clown Wheelchair Orphanage after a suspicious bazooka attack last night. It really is awful. They had so much going for them. They had just been awarded the best orphanage in Switzerland and with that received a prize for 6 million Swiss Franc! Can you guys believe that?" she said licking her lips and rubbing her hands. "Just so happened too, that because I've been working tirelessly with this great wheelchair orphanage for the past three days, they put any money received by the orphanage to go to my pie research in their owner's will. I really am so honoured."

The entire class stayed silent and began to glance over each other's shoulders after hearing how bizarre this was. Some were looking for their new classmate's expressions, some were looking for emergency fire exits.

1 hour 50 minutes into class.

"So, you see students, a bazooka still classifies as a semi-automatic. As you cannot fire it repeatedly, it must be reloaded. That is why in Switzerland, it is perfectly legal for me to own a bazooka. Even though I don't anymore. Because as I have said, I lost it last week and can't see myself finding it ever again."

Another hour after the bell rang.

"CCTV you might ask? Well yes, they did have cameras all over the orphanage. If a child fell out of their wheelchair, they would need to be found, wouldn't they? Of course they would! And it's very hard for two people, not including me, a very generous person for offering my time there might I add, to look over 16 kids in wheelchairs. CCTV is absolutely necessary! Though, unfortunately students, the CCTV was turned off the evening before the bazooka incident. Probably one of the deceased lil' rascals! However, this model of camera takes 24 hours to power back up to working again. So, no, no evidence has been brought or could be brought up." The blackboard was now covered with diagrams of 'evidence' to do with this bazooka incident and students had begun to sneak out one by one. Timmy was one of the last to do so. While Mrs. Bobbles was doing a bazooka distance demonstration by the window he left his seat as quietly as possible. He then took his hula hoop off of the door hook and left the room to see more of the college.

After dropping the hula hoop back to his room, Timmy decided to check out the campus, seeing as the place was still relatively empty. He took this time to take in the beautiful artwork around the campus. Arches as wide as pillars and pillars as long as arches. The campus was filled with unique buildings, with interesting stories. One huge skyscraper stood in the middle, with no explanation. Across from that was the pie lab where they made pies using 3 ingredients; love, magic and pie mix. Beside that was the Unicycle Workshop, where the motorheads worked on their unicycles. The quad was filled with clowns playing ultimate frisbee, Bop It and life-size Jenga. At the edge of the quad stood several liberal clowns reading the Communist Manifesto and protesting the Zionist occupation of Palestine. On the opposite side of the quad was the Clown College's neurology clinic run by the world-renowned Doctor Brainy Brian.

Modern and classical art covered the walls on both the inside and outside of the buildings. The more creative works, like 'The Pain of Comedy' by Leonardo Da Clownio, were overshadowed by the less creative work such as "The Last Supper with Clowns" as well as another modern piece of art, the painting of "Clown Dogs Playing Poker (but only using joker cards)". The statues erected in the centre of the campus caught Timmy's eye. He began to look at the masterfully crafted statues and read some of the descriptions;

'1479-1523.
Here lies 'Giuseppe El Clowno' one of the Renaissance's best entertainers. He died in 1523. Cause of death unknown. Crafted by Michaelengo'

Timmy took a step back, humbled, relishing in the fact that he had just examined a statue of the great Giuseppe El Clowno. He was also quite surprised that the whole college campus had been built on a clown burial ground. That wasn't in the brochure. Timmy brought his eyes to the next statue. This one was made of pure, solid gold. Timmy was astounded, unaware that gold could even be sculpted. The light blasted off this clown's chiseled face almost blinding Timmy. He raised his hand to block the sun and read the description;

'1621-1679.

Clownbound

Here lies 'Funzo', believed to be the original Funzo. Many documents claim Funzo to be the clown that brought down the Ming Dynasty in 1644. A roughly translated excerpt: 'when blamed for the end of the Ming Dynasty, Funzo would always say 'How would I have been able to do such a thing, I'm just a silly, powerless clown, remember?' in a tone many regarded as 'suspicious'. Crafted by unknown.'

Unaware of what the Ming Dynasty was, Timmy disregarded what he had just read and moved ever further from the campus. As he went past the exit for the college, another statue caught his eye. This one was unlike the rest of the statutes. It stood on its own, far away from any sign of life, down by the abandoned stables. Timmy decided he was in no hurry, and headed towards the old, worn down stables, with his abnormally large shoes honking every step of the way. The statue was crafted with wood, with its face smudged and unrecognisable. Timmy wiped the dust from the bottom of the statue to try read the description. It read:

*'1977-1996.
Here soon will lie Timmy Tim Tim Thompson...*

Timmy's face dropped. He froze. Terrified and confused by what he had just read, Timmy rubbed his eyes and began to read it again:

*'1977-1996.
Here soon will lie Timmy Tim Tim Thompson: The clown who knew too much. Crafted by Dippity Dancer Daniel.'*

Timmy started to panic. Endless questions flooded his mind. 'Why me?', 'Is this a prank?', 'Who is Dippity Dancer Daniel?' None of this was making any sense. Suddenly, Timmy felt a hand on his shoulder. It was a clown with a serious demeanour and goofy makeup. He handed Timmy a brown envelope, whispered, "Wibbly Wibbly Wobbly Woo!", and cartwheeled away. The front of the envelope said, 'don't open me until you're alone'. Timmy moved into the deserted barn where all the clowns sit their yearly examinations and opened the letter:

'Dear Timmy Tim Tim Thompson,

You blasted fool. Did you really think I wouldn't be able to find you? Of course you did, you were always so gullible. You probably don't know what I'm talking about, do you? Of course, the clowns don't know. Those buffoons. They have no idea. They took your 'mother' and murdered her. Justice served. 'The Rogue Clown' they called her. The Clown Bandits are the least of your worries.

I'm watching you, Timmy. If you so much as look at any of the undercover clowns and reveal what I've told you, you'll suffer immense consequences. I will be in touch again, Timmy, make no mistake about it. We will meet again. Until then, you better stay on your toes.

Regards,
Gabby-Grimly.

Timmy was shaken. It never crossed his mind that his own sibling could be the antagonist of the story. Then again, very few things made sense to Timmy these days. Timmy headed back towards his dorm room. As he walked down the hallway towards his room, #143, he could hear his roommate talking. Timmy stopped. He slowly approached the room to hear Steve talking on the phone.

"So, he got the letter? Brilliant. Don't worry, Gabby, I'll keep an eye on him. He won't suspect a thing. He even thinks I'm into this clown stuff! HA HA, I HATE clowns!" said Steve surprisingly aggressively.

Timmy felt sick. This moment confirmed one of the pieces of advice Wongo gave him before he passed: "Never trust anyone who wears glasses ah ho ho hey!"

Timmy turned around, not wanting to let Steve find out that he knew. He decided that he needed to get out of here before it's too late. He was all about funny business, but not this kind of funny business.

7: Nerds Ain't Cool

<u>An Acrobat's Catchy Pop Hit Song</u>

I love being Acrobatic-batic-batic-batic,
All you fools are static, static, static.

(instrumental)

All you fools are fake, you plastic,
Acrobatic-batic-batic-batic.

It aint hard. It aint mathematics,
Acrobatic-batic-batic-batic.

(instrumental)

And so on.

A pawn in a game of chess, Timmy felt helpless and completely out of control. His life was being thrown around like a ball in a playpen. He was part of someone else's plan and he had just about enough of the obstacles the Clown Gods were throwing his way. '*What is it to be normal,*' he pondered walking by the quad with a stiff back and searching eyes because he thought he was being watched. He went to the library where no one could harm him. Clown libraries are the loudest places on earth, what with all the goofy laughing practice. He found out Steve's timetable from the library assistants and only went back to the dorm to get some sleep when Steve had class. Luckily, Steve's classes were in blocks of nine hours a day, for his two subjects of 'Principles of balancing on a big ball' and 'An introduction to be a barber'. Timmy valued every second of rest he got, while missing a few classes here and there at the same time. It was worth it to have peace of mind.

A week had passed, and it was as if Timmy was jet lagged. His change of sleep cycle was catching up with him. He had wanted to meet up with Hybrid, but senior students didn't start until week two. A mix of his jetlag and missing Hybrid made him grumpy and yearning for home. Timmy was on his way to class, walking through a quad on campus that is advised to avoid. He walked this way to avoid Steve and it was working. Too busy looking around to see if Steve was close by, he found himself caught in the middle of a human Bop-It, where a circle of clowns surrounded him (usually 5 or 19 in the case of extreme bop-it, prison rules (Xtreme)). With thoughts flying through his mind, clowns making silly noises passing by his eyes, Timmy didn't know what was going on. He had the feeling the clowns were closing in on him and he twirled to face whichever clown was making the next noise.

Timmy's feelings were justified as the clowns were closing in with huge Happy-as-Larry expressions painted to their faces. Mouths that said fun; eyes that screamed danger. All of a sudden, the noises turned into action. This was no longer a game. Timmy didn't understand. Jocks only picked on the nerds.

'Pull it!' Timmy felted a sharp pull on his shirt and giggles emerged louder.

'Spin it!' Timmy was spun by all clowns around him at such an extreme pace he could feel the pie he had for lunch about to come back up. Through the clowns wacky and weird noises, he heard a familiar voice.

"TIMMY!" It was Hybrid, giving Timmy internal strength to endure this beating of a lifetime that was about to get worse. It did sadden him that she was watching though. He could feel it coming, the magic word. He closed his eyes preparing to take the beating of a lifetime from comically competitive clowns.

Bop it!!!

Timmy miraculously felt absolutely nothing. He heard nothing either. It was as though his senses had switched off. He was hesitant and understandably scared because he had never experienced such a thing. Even with his father he would feel every thump he had coming to him. He covered his face with his forearms. He didn't realise it, but he was still standing, although crouched and curled up into an upright ball, like when Sonic the Hedgehog is about to tuck himself into a ball. The clowns were gone. Technically they were still there, just on the ground and unconscious. Unknown to him, the events that just happened would, to Timmy's annoyance, change his life again. Almost as if Timmy's life is on a regional road in the countryside with a woman driver, trying to find a local shop for her lipstick or whatever it is they get up to.

Timmy scanned the perimeter, in search of what might have saved him. Clearing through the smoke was a large shadow figure, walking through the fog and developing into vision. About ten yards away the image became clear.

"Father!? But I thought you were dead!"

"No, that was your mother. Keep up, son."

"Don't call me son! The clown's agency told me enough about you and 'mother'."

"Oh, did they now!? Well then, I suppose these clowns must have mentioned Dippity Dancer Daniel, the infamous sculptor?" Timmy's father said with a raised eyebrow, suggesting the statement in a patronising way.

Timmy remained silent with a burning urge in his chest to attack his father in an act of revenge for the past. Luckily, he held himself back. He would soon find out why this was possibly the smartest move he could have made at the time. Holding back his anger, he looked around the building windows surrounding the quad around him. He locked eyes with Hybrid three stories above and motioned her to come down with a smile on his face. She was near tears after watching what happened to Timmy. While she was running down the stairs he turned back to his father in anger.

"Dippity Dancer Daniel? I am vaguely familiar… but tell me more!" said Timmy, tactically trying to exploit the man for more information.

"HA HA! These clowns are playing jokes on you it seems. No surprise there in fairness."

"Yeah, that's true," said Timmy looking away into the windows of the college, contemplating that this was exactly what a bunch of clowns would do. With a burst of venom, he spat on the ground in front of him. Just like that, Timmy heard his name again. It was Hybrid and she was at the bottom of the building out of breath from running down so many stairs. Timmy turned his back to his father to face her with his arms out stretched. She was wearing a long yellow dress with daisies decorated around it. The dress went down to her knees and she had daisy flipflops to go with them. Her clown make-up was put on perfectly, her fringe covering up her forehead. The makeup couldn't cover up the joy she showed when she saw Timmy.

"Get over here, ya big clown!" cried Timmy.

Hybrid took a deep breath and began to jog toward Timmy with a big smile on her face… She was glowing. Just then he heard what sounded like a small firework followed by a rush of air coming from behind him. Timmy glanced behind him to see his father crouched and looking up. Timmy looked up instinctively and saw a bazooka rocket go over his head. He then faced forward to see where it would hit. Of course, fate can be so cruel. The explosive lifted Hybrid 10ft into the air causing her to land on her back. Timmy, speechless and shaking, sprinted towards her lying on the ground. His father tried to hold him back by pulling on his shirt, but he broke free like he wasn't being pulled back at all. Brushing the stones off of her from the explosion he kept stuttering out the words "I love you," as many times as he possibly could. There was nothing else he could think of saying. He felt the heat of the rocket kneeling on the ground and the deep coolness of death setting into Hybrid. From the moment he picked her up, he didn't want to admit it, but she wasn't breathing or moving. The longer he held her, the more he could feel the slight stiffing cold effects of rigor mortis pass through her body. He knelt there wanting to die with her, but that wasn't part of the plan. His father had run over to him and picked him up over his shoulder. Timmy banged on his shoulder to put him down but that wasn't an option to his father.

His father's checked shirt was already drenched in Timmy's tears. His shoulder was bruised, and his feelings were already hurt from the names he was being called. He looked up at the building from which the rocket came. Standing inside the window with a smug look and pair of glasses was none other than the perpetrator.

"That fucking NERD!"

Timmy saw his roommate Steve reloading a bazooka that was identical to the bazooka Mrs. Bobbles had spent forty minutes describing inside and out. Maybe she was innocent after all. Steve was now looking down the scope of the bazooka, but he was out of luck. Timmy's dad had rescued him and taken him behind the bleachers of the nearby soccer stadium.

Tears flooded Timmy's face. He was in disbelief. The love of his life was murdered in cold blood right before his eyes.

"Timmy, we need to get out of here! Now!" shouted his father. 'The college has been compromised. Come with me!"

"I can't…" cried Timmy. "She was everything to me… and now she's gone… just like that…" Timmy started hyperventilating. His jaw clenched. His father was talking to him, but he couldn't hear him. His voiced mixed into the background noise. He started to feel flushed, as though all of his blood was rushing to the crown of his cranium. Suddenly, he saw red. He snatched his father's handgun from the holster and aimed it at him. "Do you have spare petrol in the car?" asked Timmy.

"Of course… I always do."

"Good," said Timmy as he went to the boot of the car. After opening it, he pulled out a container of petrol. With the petrol in his hand, he ran towards the dorm building with a look of insanity in his eyes.

Timmy made his way up to his floor, knowing he would not be satisfied until this nerd was wailed on. From the end of his hallway he saw his dorm room door swing open. Steve walked through the doorway, convinced he had completed his mission. Timmy locked eyes with him and without even thinking lunged toward him, tackling him to the ground. Timmy swung his elbow at Steve's face, shattering his glasses to pieces. With his right elbow split open from the glass, covered in blood, he swung again, slicing a cut on Steve's forehead. Directly following the elbow, Steve lunged his head forward, knocking Timmy to the ground. Timmy rolled over, holding his bloodied head. Steve slowly picked himself up. He delivered a fierce kick to Timmy's ribs, bundling him over in agony. Steve reached over to the table top for a weapon. When he turned back, Timmy was back on his feet. Steve darted a metallic blade toward Timmy's head. Timmy quickly sidestepped to the right. The blade swished by his head, stabbing the wall behind him. Timmy turned his head to see a Batman throwing knife nailed into the wall.

"Wow! You really are a fucking nerd!" said Timmy as he swung his left fist at Steve. Steve ducked his head to the right and replied with a swift punch to Timmy's already beaten up ribs. Timmy let out a roar, before pulling out his gun and shooting Steve in the knee. Steve dropped to the ground, screaming in pain.

"You cheating piece of shit!" cried Steve.

"Cheating? This was a fight... I should have pulled this out at the beginning."

"Fuck... Please... just finish me off... I'm in too much pain."

"You killed the woman I love... I want you to suffer," said Timmy as he pulled the trigger, shooting Steve's other knee. Timmy whipped out his clown lighter. He poured the petrol all over the room, leaving Steve in the centre of the room. He flicked on the lighter and threw it in the room, closing the door behind him. He ran down the stairs and out of the building without looking back.

"What did you do?" asked his father, looking at the flames forming in the building.

"Turned up the heat a little bit."

"Good God... I need you to come with me, Timmy," insisted his father.

"You can drive me to the airport... I need to go see a man about a clown."

"Where?"

"The United States!"

Clownbound

"The United States? That's a funny place to go."

"A funny place?" He took one last look at the freshly inflamed college campus surrounding him. "I should fit right in."

8: Vroom Vroom: Beep Beep!

With the flames of the Clown College burning behind them, Timmy and his father drove out of the campus onto the motorway.

"Holy shit, that was a close call! Thank God we're out of there!" said Timmy with a sigh of relief.

"Don't thank God yet, Timmy. If I know these clowns they won't give up without a fight."
Thompson then looked over his shoulder to see 6 Clown Cars bombing down the road after them. "Buckle up Timmy! It's about to be a bumpy ride!"

Thompson pushed down on the accelerator, shifted gear and put on a sweet pair of shades. Timmy was on lookout, checking how close the clowns were to them.

"We're losing them!" shouted Timmy. "Turn right here. They won't know which way we went!"

Thompson grabbed the steering wheel and swerved right.

"Whew, that was close," said Thompson as he wiped the sweat from his forehead.

The men thought they had lost the clowns, but that was a severe underestimation of the clowns. Suddenly, a Clown Motorbike came flying from over the hill and landed beside the car. There were 5 sidecars on the motorbike and each clown was laughing with AK47s in hand.

"Oh shit, not the Biker Clowns," cried Thompson who knew they were in serious trouble now. "Timmy, grab the shotgun from under your seat and blow those clowns away!"

"You got it!" Timmy shouted as he reached under, feeling for the metallic exterior of the shotgun. He was excited at the opportunity to blow some clowns. He rolled down the window.

"Get slammed you hilarious looking motherfuckers," roared Timmy as he put his head out the window and shot the front wheel of the motorbike. The bike flipped. All of the clowns got thrown from their seats. All of them, except one. One of the clowns managed to get a hold of the top of their car. He stood on top, pretending to be surfing on the car. Timmy and Thompson appreciated how funny that must have looked outside of this context.

"This clown's mine, Timmy!" Thompson adjusted himself and climbed out the window. "Grab the wheel!" Thompson reached the roof of the car and pulled out his nunchucks.

"HAHAHA," laughed the clown as he pulled out his machete. "You think you can beat me? HAHAHA you must be joking me!"

Thompson took off his shades. "I'm not the clown. I don't do jokes," said Thompson as he flexed on the clown.

The area on top of the car was small, leaving little room for a misstep. The clown rushed at Thompson, swinging his machete like a baseball bat. Thompson dipped and rolled around him. Thompson leaned in and wrapped the nunchucks around the clowns' legs, pulling him to the ground. With an incredible kip up, the clown got back to his feet. The clown reefed the nunchucks off Thompson and threw them off the car, causing two cars to collide head on and blow up. Thompson got back up.

"Okay, now this is personal, clown!" said Thompson as he roundhouse kicked the clown in the head. Quickly, before the clown could respond with a follow-up, Thompson swiftly punched him in the liver, forcing the clown to drop his machete. Thompson lifted the clown over his head and shouted, "How's this for a balancing act?" He threw the clown into another clown bike causing 5 more clowns to be flung from their seats. Thompson hopped back into the car and took over the driving.

"That sounded pretty intense!" said Timmy. "But, ehhh, that 'balancing act' line was kinda weak."

"What was that?" said Thompson who couldn't hear Timmy over the sound of clowns roaring in pain and laughter out the window.

"Oh, I just said good job!" lied Timmy, realising now was not the time to call out his father's choice of language.

Timmy glanced out the window and saw that there were no clowns in sight. But he could sense this fight was far from over. Within a minute another Clown Car appeared behind them. This one looked different.

"What's that on the roof of the Clown Car?" said Timmy with a worried tone.

Thompson looked in the rear-view mirror. "Oh, dear God no. They have a Clown Cannon. I'm going to need you to get on top of the roof and make sure no clowns get in this car!"

Without even thinking, Timmy grabbed the shotgun and another machine gun from the back and climbed out the window. The first clown from the cannon flew by the driver seat window, just missing the car. "Zooooiiiiiiinks!" screamed the clown as he crashed to the ground, snapping his neck and dying instantly.

'*That was close,*' thought Timmy. Not wanting another close call, he loaded up the machine gun and started gunning down the Clown Car. Bullets ripped through the Clown Car, causing the car to flip over. All 36 of the clowns in the car went flying with the car. Timmy jumped back into the passenger seat, certain that there were no more Clown Cars to come. Thompson pulled up outside a long field with a single plane in it.

Clownbound

"Timmy, I need you to get in that plane and watch this when you do." Thompson handed Timmy a brown bag with a VHS tape inside it. "Go quick! No time to explain, son, just go!"

Timmy grabbed the bag and jumped out of the car. He walked towards the plane. He looked behind him and could see Clown Cars in the distance.

"Quick son! Get on the plane now! Run!" screamed Thompson.

Timmy ran to the plane with a tear in his eye. Timmy was the only one on the plane, other than the pilots. His seat had a VHS recorder set up in front of him. He put the VHS tape in the machine and sat back in anticipation. The screen turned on and Timmy saw his father sitting in front of the camera with a sad look on his face.

"Hello son... if you're watching this then you made it to the plane and the clowns have gotten me."

Timmy paused the video, confused by the accuracy of the statement. He shrugged his shoulders and pressed play.

"There's a lot I should have told you, Timmy. Leaving you uninformed is one of my biggest regrets. This plane is not heading for the US, its headed for Peru. I need you to meet somebody in Machu Picchu. You see son... Not all the clowns are bad. In fact, there are an organisation of clowns that are trying to change the world for the better. You will meet them in Peru and they will further explain the situation. Timmy, I am so sorry I wasn't there for you and I am proud of you." Timmy paused the tape again as he was flooded with tears. He wiped his eyes and thought to himself *I knew all clowns weren't bad.*

The tape continued, "I must tell you the story of Dippity Dancer Daniel, son. I must tell you how we wound up living

in Yugoslavia. This is a long story and it starts back in the
early 1970s..."

<u>A Chimpanzee's Attempt</u>

EEWWEEWWEEWW
AHHAHHAHHHAAHH

EEWWEEWWEEWW
AHHAHHAHHHAAHH

EEWWEEWWEEWW
AHHAHHAHHHAAHH

EEWWEEWWEEWW
AHHAHHAHHHAAHH

09/03/1971 – Vietnam

In 1963, following the assassination of John F. Kennedy, 16000 American military personnel had set up camp in South Vietnam. Two years later the first group of U.S. Marines were dispatched to South Vietnam. Six years following the arrival of these 3500 men, the most classified squadron in US history arrived. They were set with task C.L.O.W.N: Capture "Loopy Oak" With Net. Loopy Oak was the most notorious clown since Silly Samuel, Adolf Hitler's personal clown. Loopy was wanted by the US Government on charges of treason, murder, and several unpaid fines for the unsafe, overfilling of cars. He fled from the US to Vietnam sixteen years previously, in January 1955. Some believe Loopy Oak to be the cause of the Vietnam War, however, when questioned about this JFK would always respond with, "I'm not going to even answer that, because that is so fucking stupid."

Team C.L.O.W.N arrived on the coast of Vietnam, nets in hand. The team consisted of five well-trained soldiers; Joseph Moore, Roger Thompson, Daniel Smith, Timothy Harris and Jose Rodriguez.

"So, here we are!" announced the team leader, Joseph Moore. "There will be no sleeping tonight boys. Grab some food and get hydrated, we're moving in T-minus 2 hours."

"I hope somebody brought some tacos ayyy," said the lovable Jose Rodriquez.

When everybody eventually stopped laughing, they sat down by the campfire and started eating beans.

"You're awful quiet, stretch," snarked Timothy in Daniel's direction. "What age are you anyway, kid? You look like you should be starting high school!"

Daniel laughed. "I'm a bit of an artist." he said as he continued to eat.

"I'm not sure what that means or what that adds to the conversation but okay. What about you?" remarked Timothy as he looked in the direction of the absolute bear that was Roger Thompson.

"Well, you know I just thought going to war would beat the hell out of sitting at home all day doing diddly squat," said Thompson with a smile. He looked down and hesitated. "I do miss my girl though, I'll admit that!"

"Ayyy homes I miss her too," quipped Jose.

"You're such a clown!" laughed Timothy, as he smacked his leg. Suddenly, Daniel looked incredibly uncomfortable. He got up and walked away from the group.

"What's his problem?" asked Thompson.

"Must be afraid of clowns ayyyyyy!" laughed the delightful Jose.

"God damn Rodriguez, you crack me up!" said all the other men in unison.

"Nah but I feels you, homes. I miss my wife and kids too," said Jose. He took a photo of his family out of his wallet and handed it to Thompson. "You got any kids?"

Timothy shook his head as Thompson said, "Nah I ain't got any kids at the moment. I'm only 18. But I plan on having them at least in the next 20 years ha ha!"

"You should name your firstborn after me!" laughed Timothy.

"Yeah, that'll be the day."

"Alright men! Grab your nets, we're heading for the top of the mountain. Intel tells us that's where Loopy Oak is hiding!" shouted Moore as he headed into the forest.

The men packed up and followed Moore into the forest. Moore led the way with Timothy, Roger and Jose right behind him, deep in discussion. The shy, introvert looking Daniel followed behind them.

"So, Timothy, you're asking a lot of questions! We gotta know what your backstory is, huh?" said Thompson with a teasing tone.

"Yeah bro what is you hiding ayyy," laughed the charming Jose.

"Alright alright, I'll spill. This is very secret though, so you guys better not rat me out," said Timothy with an unusual tone of seriousness.

"Go on," said the two men, clearly very interested in what Timothy was about the say.

"Okay... I'm an undercover Vietnamese spy," joked Timothy in a stereotypical Vietnamese accent.

Timothy and Thompson laughed as Thompson gave him a playful dig. "Gosh dang it, Timothy, you had me going there!"

"Sorry boys, I had to! And call me Timmy. We're all friends here," said Timothy.

"Ayy, I don't know, homes. That was a bit distasteful and a cheap attempt at crude humour, if I'm being honest," added Jose, a man who was not a fan of stereotypes.

An hour into the hike they reached the bottom of the mountain. It wasn't a particularly daunting climb, but a fall from the top would kill you on impact. The five men stood in awe as the average sized mountain loomed before them. Cold grey crevices held the blood of many battles. The lower passes of the mountain wore a cloak of greenery, while the peaks were crowned with a headdress of ice. Without a word passing between them, the men knew they had a task ahead of them. The men began climbing. The enthusiastic Jose led the way on the climb, followed by Timothy and Thompson. Below them was Daniel, with Moore at the bottom. As Jose reached the top of the icy mountain, Timothy began to struggle. His hands were covered in sweat, making the last few minutes of the climb feel like an eternity. As he reached for Jose's hand at the top of the mountain, he heard a roar.

"HELP!"

Thompson froze, knowing this could only mean trouble. He looked below him and saw Daniel hanging from the edge of the mountain, barely holding on. Moore was nowhere to be seen.

"Hold on! I'm coming for you," shouted Thompson as he lowered himself to help Daniel up the mountain. Daniel's hand slipped and as he saw his life flash before his eyes, he felt a firm grasp suspend him from 40 feet. He looked up at Thompson who had timed his catch to perfection.

"I owe you a life, Thompson!" said Daniel in disbelief.

"What the fuck happened? Where's Moore? Did he fall?" demanded Timothy, clearly fazed by what he had just experienced.

"I don't know. He just fell. Maybe he slipped," said Daniel, unconvincingly.

"Fuck. Where do we go now?" asked Timothy.

"Ayyy the top of the mountain is right there," said Jose. "How's about we finish the job and head there now!"

The men began to head towards the top of the mountain, all very shaken by the loss of Moore. Leading the way, Jose reached the top of the mountain and stopped.

"Ayy hol'up, no mames! Son unas mamadas!" said Jose in an even more pronounced Mexican accent.

Timothy and Thompson stood there in shock, as they looked at the silly looking oak tree that stood in front of them. They sighed and placed their hands on their heads trying to figure out what had happened.

Timothy and Thompson sat down silently on the ground, both feeling defeated.

"Yo homes, did yous hear that spooky sound?" said Jose as he stood dead still trying to hear more.

"Hear what?" asked both the men.

"Ayyo Shhh," whispered Jose. "Listen."

The men started listening intensely to try hear what Jose thought he heard.

"HONK!"

"Woah what the fuck was that," said Timothy, startled.

"HONK HONK HONK HONK!"

The noise grew louder as the men began to back up. When suddenly from behind the tree appeared a three-wheeled, red car. The back door of the car opened. A clown jumped out, juggling three bottles and whistling the US national anthem.

Within a minute, 15 clowns exited the car and surrounded the men.

"Oh sweet Jesus, no," said Thompson as he swung the net towards the clowns.

"Which one of you is Loopy Oak?" demanded Jose.

And with that Jose felt a metal square push up against the back of his head.

"Loopy Oak... HAHAHA Loopy Oak!? Don't you know... don't you know who I am? Loopy Oak is a hoax! Look at that tree in front of you. That's a loopy oak you absolute fucking idiots. No no. I'm not Loopy Oak. You can call me Dippity Dancer Daniel."

Thompson was in shock when he turned around and saw little Daniel holding a gun to Jose's head.

"This war is merely a patch of dirt on the real field of life. The US Government and the Vietnamese Government are pawns, you fools. You pledged your lives to a cause that doesn't even matter. The governments, the corporations, none of them matter. They are not running the world. We are. To compare a politician to a clown or magician is to compare a peasant to God himself."

The fan favourite Jose's eyes began to water, "Thompson, tell my wife and keeds I love them!"

Daniel laughed, took a step back and pulled the trigger. Blood splattered all over Timothy who dropped to the ground in tears. Daniel then turned to Timothy and shot him in the chest. Surrounded by more than a dozen clowns, Thompson didn't know what to do.

"Why? Why are you doing this, Daniel?" begged Thompson.

"Why? HA! I'd be a fool to give away my plans!"

"Well isn't 'fool' just another word for clown?"

Clownbound

"Huh!" Dippity Dancer Daniel stopped to think about this for a minute. "I suppose it is… Alright fine, I'll tell you my plans. You see Thompson, none of this matters. The Americans, the Vietnamese… They're not important. This war… It's gibble gosh, it's trivial, it's the crust of the cake. I'm a Mercenary Clown, Thompson. I'm paid to assassinate presidents, tear down dynasties and tie animal balloons together. I did it all for the money. It was always for the money; that sweet coin, that wonga, the dollar strut! And I was paid to take out both the United States and Vietnam by the chim—" Dippity Dancer Daniel stopped. "It's not important who paid me. But sometimes," he paused and let out a sigh, "sometimes money isn't enough. I was one phone call away from destroying both countries and I thought to myself, *'Why are you doing this Daniel? You already have all the money a clown could ever wish for.'* And I was right, I did! Somewhere down the line money just lost its hold on me. You can only buy so many rhino horns and loom bands. But I discovered what I was really after. I discovered where the true value lies. Power. Power over others and power over all. So, I, the leader of the Mercenary Clowns, am going to gather an army of clowns, magicians, and even contortionists and we're going to overthrow the entire Circus Empire. But we'll be slick. We'll be smooth. Nobody will even notice. I'll slowly climb the political ladder. Sure, it'll be hard. My mercenaries can't be trusted. They're mercenaries after all, a bunch of snakes! But they couldn't stop me if they tried. I'm destined to go up the ladder. It's the only way I can win, and even though it's a roll of the dice, I like my odds. But I'll avoid the snakes and climb the ladder all the way to the top, something a Mercenary Clown would never have dreamed of doing, and once I'm at the top I'll chop the heads off all the carnies and my reign will commence. How's that for a plan?"

"Fairly comprehensive," admitted Thompson.

"I'm going to let you live, Thompson, because what's a clown without his honour? But only on one condition. You cannot mention this to anybody. I will have you relocated to Yugoslavia and you will start a new life there. But Thompson we will be watching you. I'll have my best spy on the case. If you slip up, we will know, and we WILL ruin your life! So, Thompson. You better not slip..."

Thompson stood there with his jaw dropped as the 15 clowns grabbed him and squeezed him into the Clown Car.

10: The Truth Part Deux

As the plane flew through the clouds, Timmy was struggling to come to grips with reality. He had just lost the love of his life and his father; someone he was only on the horizon of understanding. After a twelve-hour flight, the plane landed on the Peruvian mountaintop. As Timmy left the plane, he felt the air become arctic cold. Goosebumps formed on his forearm. His body began to shake with the cold. Clouds swirled around him. Grass coated the mountaintop.

"Here," said the pilot, "you might want these." He handed Timmy a heavy woollen jumper, a pair of fingerless gloves and a hat with the words 'Bad Bitchez Only' inscribed on it. Timmy quickly threw on this new apparel.

"Is there a reason the gloves are fingerless?" asked Timmy.

"I think it's just the way they were designed," said the pilot.

"No, I mean why didn't you give me gloves with fingers?"

"With fingers? What?"

"Not literal fingers... Like, normal gloves and not fingerless gloves..."

"Look kid, I don't know. I'm a pilot, not a fashion enthusiast."

"It's not really a question of fashion. It's common sense. I'm not trying to be an asshole or anything, but why give me gloves with less protection? Its freezing cold here."

"Well, how do you think I feel?" said the pilot, who was wearing shorts. Timmy shrugged as if to say, 'fair enough' and went to look down from where they landed.

"So, this is Peru?" said Timmy as he looked down from the summit.

"Yep," said the pilot.

"It's beautiful!"

"You too."

"What?"

"I said sure is."

"Right. So, what exactly am I supposed to do now?"

"What do you mean?"

"Well, I was told I'd be met by people here."

"Oh yeah!"

"And?"

"And what?

"Where are they?"

"See… I'm not sure."

"What do you mean you're not sure?"

"As in, like, I'm not certain. Look I'm a pilot okay? What happens on land has nothing to do with me. The sky? That's my house. If something is going wrong up there, I'm your man."

"Alright then mister pilot… Are they late?"

"Possibly."

"Well, are we early? Or late?"

The pilot glanced at his watch, "No, no, we're on time. We timed it pretty well actually, if you don't mind me saying."

"So, they're late?"

"Could be."

"Right…" said Timmy. He was beginning to get frustrated. He couldn't tell if the pilot was being annoying on purpose or if there was genuinely something wrong with him.

Suddenly, a figure on a horse appeared from beyond a palm tree south of where they were standing. The horse galloped towards Timmy and the pilot. The horse had a red nose and his mane was dyed the colours of the rainbow. The clown pulled the horse to a stop. He hopped off the horse and approached them. He took off his glasses, put his hand into his pocket and pulled out a monocle. After placing the monocle on his right eye, he leaned towards Timmy, scanning his entire body. The clown turned towards the pilot. "Is this the boy?" asked the clown in his best Alan Rickman impression. The pilot nodded. The clown read the words on Timmy's hat. "Hell yeah ha ha!" he said, going in for a fist bump.

"My name is Señor Silly Sr. It is my duty to bring you, Timmy Tim Tim Thompson, to the great Tomb of Peru."

"Wow. Right… Okay…"

"Before you take the boy," started the pilot, "you must recite the agreed upon code."

"With pleasure," said Señor Silly. "Zippity Zoopity Zappity Zap!"

The pilot nodded again and turned away, walking back toward the plane.

"Now come with me, young Timmy!"

"Yessir."

Señor Silly Sr helped Timmy onto the horse. With both men on horseback, Señor Silly let out a whistle, prompting the horse to gallop back through the mountaintop. The horse neighed as his hooves clicked and clacked. They continued to click and clack as they brushed through the greenery.

"What was with those clowns back in Zurich? Why were they attacking my father and I?"

"They were Mercenary Clowns. Or Bandit Clowns. The worst type of clown. Apart from politicians, that is. But these clowns were paid off by the Magicians."

"Magicians?"

"Yes, the Magicians."

"Why me?"

"We're not sure… whoever is in charge of the Magicians at the moment obviously knows you somehow."

"Why are the Magicians turning on the Clowns in the first place?"

"They want to collect all th—" he paused. "The why is not important, young Timmy. What's important is that these Magicians are a danger to us all! You must tread lightly at all times. They could be anywhere, disguised as anybody."

"How do I know you aren't a Magician then?"

"Because I'm not."

"But that's exactly what they would say!"

"Have you ever met a Magician?"

"No."

"So, how in Clown's name would you know that's what they would say?"

"I don't know. That's just something I've seen people say in the movies and all."

"Is this a movie, Timmy?"

"No..."

"Alright, how about you shut up then, yeah?"

"Okay…"

"Anyway. With the Circus Olympics just around the corner we cannot afford to lose any more clowns. Will you be competing?"

"I can't. I never graduated Clown College, so I don't have my 'Crazy Clown Certificate.'

"A degree is not the only route to Clownhood, Timmy."

"What do you mean?"

"There are many ways one can become a clown. The easiest way is through bloodline. If your parents were clowns, then you would have a spot waiting for you upon birth. If this doesn't apply to you, then you could take the long route. Climb the Circus ladder. You could start off as a pathetic part-time clown who works children's parties. From there you audition for local Circuses and hope one will take you on. This one is very unlikely, though. If I ran a Circus there would be no way I would hire one of those 'clowns'. Don't make me sick. Another route would be through the Circus school systems, but that is only available to those under 18. In times of dire need there can be a Clown Ceremony to see if one is worthy of being a clown. This is rare, but sometimes it's the only way. And the final route is through nomination. You must be nominated by somebody in the knowhow."

"Another clown?"

"Not necessarily. It could be somebody the clowns have great respect for. For example, somebody like Gandhi or Sylvester Stallone." The horse continued to gallop through the clouds. Timmy looked around him and took in the incredibly detailed scenery.

"Who are they?" asked Timmy as three men approached on camelback. Señor Silly suddenly brought the horse to a stop.

"This is where my journey ends. Go forth, Timmy. These men will take you to the Tomb. Be quick. He is waiting."

"Who is?" asked Timmy. Without a reply, Señor Silly and his horse faded into the background.

"Are you the three wise men?" joked Timmy, as the three men on camelback approached.

"No. But… I LOVED that joke!" said one of the men.

"Is that sarcasm?"

"No, I LOVED it!"

"Right…"

"HA HA three wise men!!! Like the Biblical story!!"

Timmy leaned into one of the other men and said, "What's his problem? Why is he so easily amused?"

"That's Chuckles. He just *really* likes his job. He's not the best clown, but Jesus Christ does he love clown humour. One time I hit him with the hand buzzer gag, and he didn't stop laughing for three weeks. Three weeks! Just nonstop laughter for three weeks. And I have to share a room with him."

"To be fair, that buzzer gag is genius! I was in stitches laughing when I first got it!"

"Yeah... The first time. This was like the fifth time I did it to him. Fifth and last. He laughs more every time. That's the weirdest part."

"Right..." said Timmy. "So, will I hop on the back of one of your camels?"

"No. Walk beside us," said the third clown.

"Oh, okay."

Timmy and the three Camelback Clowns made their way towards an enormous opening in the mountain. The opening was filled with other clowns, standing upright with guns in hand. Less than 100 metres into the opening stood a huge wall. A door stood in the middle, with torches lit on either side.

"This is as far as we go, Timmy," said one of the Camelback Clowns.

"Really? What was the point of that? I mean Señor Silly Sr easily could have taken me the extra 5 minutes it took to get here. I don't even know your names. Except for Chuckles of course."

"That's just the way it goes."

"I don't get it. Are you all going to come back?"

"Nope."

"Right... That was pointless. I was certain the camels had something to do with something."

"Like what?"

"I don't know… It felt like there was some sort of joke I was missing."

"Look kid. We're just trying to do our job."

"Fair enough. So, I just go this way?" asked Timmy, as he pointed towards the door.

"Yep," said one of the clowns. He then took out a whip and smacked the camel on the side while shouting, "Yup ya boya!"

Timmy reached the megalithic door, 40 times the size of an average door. He looked around him to see hundreds of Security Clowns standing in lines with straight faces. Behind these clowns were the rocky walls of the deep cave. These walls were covered with tiki torches and signs saying, 'This way to the big man.'

Summoning up the courage for a joke, Timmy said, "What is that? A door for giants?"

The joke was a success as the group gasped with laughter. Some of the clowns fell to the ground with laughter. They rolled in agony as they tried to come out of the laughter fit.

"A door for giants? HA HA YES! Who is this kid? He's incredible!" shouted one of the clowns. Many of the clowns managed to pull themselves up, however, three clowns did not make it.

"He is going to love you!" laughed the Chief Clown Security Guard.

"Who?" Timmy said with absolute confusion.

"Me!" echoed a voice from the above stairway.

THOMP THOMP THOMP

Thunderous footsteps came from the stairways. A whiff of too much aftershave filled the cave as the man reached the entrance of the door. What stood before Timmy was the mightiest clown he had ever laid eyes on.

Clownbound

All the clowns dropped to their knees. The flames on the walls were put out from the forceful wind of the voice that travelled through the humongous hall.

"Who are you?" shouted Timmy with curiosity and bravery.

"Who am I? Let me tell you. I am the King of Clowns. I am the biggest clown in the world. I am Ronald Drump" roared the monstrous voice. "And I know why you are here, young Timmy."

"Oh yeah? Why am I here?"

"Answers! You want answers! The reason you are here… dates all the way back to the war of the Magicians and Clowns. World War 1 and a half!"

11: The Illusion

<u>The Men who Wear Stilt's Long Poem</u>

It's 1910,
We've just been defeated.

No fault of our own,
The chimps have cheated.

We had the lead,
In the unicycle race.

We took off fast,
We set the pace.

In the last stretch,
We thought we had it won.

Stilts would make history,
Tonight we'd drink rum.

God, we hate them,
Chimpanzee audience got loose.

Event was called off,
Security made us vamoose.

This is a day,
We'll never forget.

Clownbound

The people with stilts,
You'll wish you never met.

"Wow, just wow!" Timmy took a step back, flabbergasted. "What an amazing story with incredibly detailed fight scenes and some of the best character development ever documented."

"Yes, quite," proudly replied Ronald Drump, who had just revealed the whole story of the war between the Magicians and Clowns.

"Truly a story worthy of its own chapter in some book, if not a whole book or even a movie dedicated to it!" said Timmy, still astounded by the amazing story.

"But, young Timmy, I hope you take what I told you seriously! These Magicians are not to be messed with! Their ability to trick people can be deadly, as you know from what I told you about what the Magicians did to the clowns in the 'Gibraltar Siege.'"

Timmy vomited all over himself for the second time, thinking about the 'Gibraltar Siege' story again. "Good God, it's even worse the second time you think about it! Those poor monkeys... I swear I won't fall for their illusions.

"Good." Ronald Drump faked a smile, knowing Timmy did not possess the power to avoid what these Magicians were capable of.

"By the way, is there somewhere for me to sleep tonight?" questioned Timmy, clearly worried.

"HA HA! Don't fret young Timmy, we have a room for you! But now is not the time for sleeping... Now is the time to officially initiate you into the Coordinated Cooky Clown Committee!" said Drump as he limbo-ed out of the room.

"Wait, what? I'm not ready! I thought I'd at least get a full night sleep first!" cried Timmy as he chased after Drump.

Timmy jogged after him into the next room, a room filled with ceremonial clown decorations and clowns dancing.

"He is here! He is ready... He. Is. Clown," shouted Drump. This was met with a cheer from all the other clowns, who continued to dance. The High Clown of Peru walked into the room with the Ceremonial Clown Cat, who was dressed as a clown.

"Hilarious," said Timmy. "That cat looks absolutely hilarious."

All the clowns gathered around the centre of the room, dancing to a slightly less intensity than before.

"Let us begin," announced the High Clown of Peru, one of only 6 remaining High Clowns. "Timmy, come to me young man. It is time for the Crazy Clown Ceremony."

Timmy walked through all the clowns and onto the podium in the centre of the room. A large apple tree stood beside the podium. Bells started to ring as the room went dead silent.

"We are gathered here today to welcome a new clown to the Guild of Clowns. We will now ask the 'Clown Questions'," said the High Clown. "Timmy Tim Tim Thompson, first of your name, do you pledge to dedicate yourself to the cause of the clowns?" asked the High Clown.

"Yessir," replied Timmy.

"And Timmy Tim Tim Thompson, first of your name, do you swear to never wear anything that isn't clown related for the rest of your days?"

"Yessir."

"And finally, Timmy Tim Tim Thompson, first of your name, will you pledge to protect the updock?"

"What's updock?" asked Timmy, who started to laugh after he realised what he said. "Ha ha, brilliant!"

Clownbound

The High Clown opened the drawer beside the podium and took out a pile of wrinkled sheets bound in the finest leather known to man. It was 'The Book of Clowns'. All clowns must place a hand on this book and swear their lives to the cause of the clowns. This was the penultimate part of the ceremony.

"Young Timmy, place your hand on this ancient book and recite the Clown Creed."

Timmy moved his hand on top of the frail book and began:

"I, Timmy Tim Tim Thompson, believe in the one true Clown.

The maker of Heaven and Earth,

of all things hilarious and silly.

Clown from Clown, circus from circus,

The one true Clown to the one true Clown,

On this day I offer you my soul.

On this day I give you my future.

Despite being a mere mortal,

I ask you on this day...

Maketh me become Clown."

"Excellent. Now Timmy you must grab one of the sacred Clown Fruits from the ancient, portable Clown Apple Tree. Once you do, we will truly find out if you are clown or not."

Timmy reached for the apple closest to him. Suddenly, he felt a hand on his shoulder.

"No, Timmy. Not that apple. We don't do low hanging fruit here," said Drump the clown.

"Oh okay, sorry…" Timmy jumped and swiped one of the higher hanging apples. "What do I do now?"

"Bite the apple, son."

"Okay…" Timmy took a bite of the apple.

"Well?" asked the High Clown of Peru.

"Well what?"

"How does it taste?"

"Like an apple…"

"Good. Very good."

Timmy looked around, confused. He stopped and took a breath. Suddenly a light shone around him as all the clowns surrounding him fell to their knees. A voice from the heavens filled the room.

"You're in," echoed the voice.

Timmy gasped and began to tear up.

"He is CLOWN!" shouted the High Clown. "The ceremony has been completed."

All the surrounding clowns began to dance again. Timmy knew tonight was going to be a crazy night.

Timmy walked into the party room which was filled with party balloons and several portraits of the same gorilla. Everybody was dancing at a higher intensity now. The music was so loud that he couldn't even hear himself think.

'Wow, I can't even hear myself think,' he thought. *'What?'* he then thought.

Timmy weaved his way through the crowds of champagne-baring chimpanzee waiters and dancing clowns. He made his way up to the balcony overlooking the dancefloor, where he was greeted by Drump.

"Ah young Timmy, a clown at last. How does it feel?" asked Drump as he handed Timmy a golden ring.

"Words can't do it justice Mr Drump!" responded Timmy, as he placed the ring on his finger without question. He then grabbed a glass of champagne from one of the well-dressed chimpanzees.

"I take it you're excited for the Circus Olympics next month? You know, Timmy... Every clown is expected to participate in the Circus Olympics and represent the clowns in their first year. I'll train you. You know what? We'll start tomorrow."

"Yessir. It's just with everything going on, I thought they might cancel it," said Timmy.

"NONSENSE!" roared Drump. "I'll be rolling in my grave before the Circus Olympics ever ends. It predates the 'normal' Olympics and is an integral part of our identity. This isn't the first time there has been conflict between the clowns and the Magicians, Timmy. During the war we set aside our differences and celebrated the 730th Circus Olympics in Brussels. As evil as the Magicians are, they would never commit atrocities during the Circus Olympics. They have their limits."

Timmy took to the dancefloor, excited about the prospect of winning gold in the Circus Olympics. He began to throw some shapes in every which direction, impressing some of the other clowns.

"You're a pretty good dancer, Timmy. But can you do this?" asked one of the clowns, who proceeded to move his body to the beat. He put his right foot forward and his left foot back and he started clowning down.

"You mean like this?" said Timmy, as he began clowning down to the beat.

"Now you're getting it!" responded the clown, who started to do the worm.

Timmy was having the night of his life! The spotlight was on him and he loved it. He had come a long way from the tiny, timid boy who went to the circus the first time.

Suddenly, the music stopped. The room went completely dark.

"What's going on?" demanded Drump. Everybody was panicking until eventually the room went dead quiet. The light came back on. Gasps filled the room as the High Clown of Peru's body was hanging from the ceiling.

"TA-DA," screeched a voice from the opposite side of the room.

"Oh, sweet Clown, no," announced Drump. "Timmy, the Magicians are here. We need to leave before they begin their illusions!"

It was too late. The doors were sealed, and the clowns were surrounded by the Magicians. They began to slaughter every second clown, leaving a river of blood pouring from the mountain of bodies.

"Timmy Tim Tim Thompson... I told you I would find you."

Timmy looked behind him to see a tall, dark figure approach him.

"Gabby... You... You rat bastard. You were a Magician this whole time! You paid Steve to try kill me, didn't you?!"

"Damn right I did! I think he needs a new pair of glasses because he clearly failed!"

"You monster... I hate you! Don't tell me you're going to be at the Circus Olympics?" asked Timmy with serious concern.

"You're damn right I'll be at the Circus Olympics, and I'm taking home the gold, baby," said Gabby, who was dressed in a female tuxedo with a top hat and cape.

"Well you failed here!" spat Timmy. "Most of the clowns already left after the ceremony. You've only got the dancing clowns!"

"It is not these clowns we want, Timmy. We want Drump. Dead." Gabby pointed her wand at Drump. Drump backflipped off the balcony, avoiding the deadly spell that was cast upon him.

Timmy jumped down after Drump. They saw an exit and darted for it. As Timmy approached the exit, he heard a roar.

"TIMMY!"

He turned. His heart sank as he almost fainted. He couldn't believe what his eyes were seeing.

"Hybrid?" cried Timmy, as he fell to his knees. He could see Hybrid, alive and breathing, being held at wandpoint by Gabby.

"Please Timmy save me. I want to go back to trapezing!" cried Hybrid.

"She's not real! She's an illusion!" shouted Drump. But it was worthless. Timmy was frozen. He knew it couldn't be real, but he wanted to believe so badly that he couldn't think straight.

"I love you so much, Timmy. I haven't gone a day without thinking about you. Please don't let them kill me!" cried Hybrid, who died yesterday.

'What do you want? I'll do anything! What do you want from me, Gabby!?'

Gabby looked at Drump, who was standing between Timmy and the exit. 'Hand him and the ring over and we'll let her go!'

Timmy turned to Drump.

"It's just an illusion, Timmy. I'm sorry, but she's gone for good," begged Drump.

Timmy turned his face to Gabby, covered in tears. He put his hand in his pocket and pulled out an oval shaped object.

"She hated trapezing," shouted Timmy as he threw the grenade on the ground and tackled Drump out of the exit. The explosion completely blocked the exit. Timmy and Drump ran away towards the sunset, as Gabby's voiced echoed out to them.

"See you at the Circus Olympics, Timmy!"

12: If it Ain't Plank, I Ain't Walkin' it

"Well where the hell did that come from!?" Timmy yelled at Drump with unblinking, scared eyes.

"Where did that come from? You! You fool! They must have put a 'tracking rabbit in a hat device' on that plane," Drump said with disgust while still coughing up blood. They were still not far from the sacred location of Clown. This meant they had no time to rest. Drump marched over to Timmy with fury and passion and reefed him up from the rock he was sitting on. "Was anyone on that plane wearing a hat, boy!?"

"Eh…Yeah sure the pilot was! Was it him?" said Timmy struggling to get his emotions and words in order.

"Of course it was him! Unless there were other people wearing other hats were there?"

"No."

"Well obviously it was him then wasn't it!" spat Drump.

The two clowns had just come from the Clown Ceremony, but what had just happened involved no funny business. In fact, because of the lavish party it wasn't even profitable business. Overall, it was bad business. They needed to get somewhere safe as soon as possible. If they didn't, the Magicians would imprison them quicker than they could say "abracadabra". Jumping between trees and hiding in bushes, Timmy was struggling to keep his composure. He was incredibly nervous and had no idea what the plan was. He was afraid to ask. It was clear Drump was pissed off. Their silent and slightly tense journey continued until the pair stopped at the entrance of a forest filled with trees up to 100-feet tall. The leaves of the trees covered the night sky and fireflies were all that guided them. The sounds of Magicians beckoned in the distance, "Zap", "Zip" and "Zoop".

"Come on. Follow me closely," whispered Drump.

They crouched and jumped between trees to remain unseen. Drump lowered his hands to the ground. He dragged his hands along the ground as they continued along the forest. Timmy was perplexed. *'Have I been left with a madman?'* he thought. After about five minutes, the pair were close enough to the source of the noise. They could now see brightly shining wands swinging in the distance. Sweat began to form in the palms of Timmy's hands and on his forehead. With a finger pressed up against his lips to urge Timmy to be quieter, Drump turned around to the gang of travelling Magicians once more. Timmy watched over his shoulder to see how Drump would handle this. With his left hand, Drump pulled out six rabbits which he had gathered when he was gliding his hand along the ground. After he pulled the finger from his lips, he reached into his other pocket and pulled out a greyhound. He held it by the muzzle, ensuring it would not make noise. A clown's trouser pockets are similar to Clown Cars in that they're made to hold both more than people would expect and they're also both very stylish.

Drump let the rabbits loose. They hopped around slowly, eating grass. But as soon as the greyhound was let loose, they began to pick up speed. All of them dashed in front of the Magicians, immediately catching the attention of all of them. Rabbits are to Magicians like bins are to bin men or bricks are to brick people. One cannot live without the other. The twelve Magicians split the group, two per rabbit, except for two lone rangers that wandered off on their own, attempting to come back as a hero to the other Magicians. Drump saw the smaller and more vulnerable one. He was to be Drump's victim. The Magician was already breathing heavily as he was running through the knee-high grass chasing after the rabbit. They moved closer to the Magician, standing only a few metres behind him. Drump pulled a taser out of his pocket. He snuck directly behind the Magician before smacking him in the back of the head with the taser, knocking him unconscious.

Drump threw the KO'd Magician over his shoulder and motioned Timmy to follow him.

After about two miles Timmy stopped, looked up at Drump with eyes full of defeat and said, "No more. My legs are cramping up beyond belief, sir."

"Suck it up, Timmy. We're almost there anyway!"

After another five minutes of walking they reached a boat-shaped cottage surrounded by a small moat. The building was one of the most unusual buildings Timmy had ever seen. He didn't understand how someone living in a fake ship could help them.

"Are you sure this is the right place?" asked Timmy.

"Absolutely. Look into the water if you don't believe me."

Timmy gazed into the narrow moat guarding the house. He saw several clownfish swimming and jumping and thought, *'Okay, we're safe.'* Drump went to open the door without knocking. His attempt was stopped after a few inches by a chain lock.

"What ARRGHHHHH yee doing down 'ere!?" demanded someone from behind the door.

"It's me, Drump! We need a place to lay low for a while. Sorry for not knocking. We didn't have time."

"Drump? Well, do yee have an offering?"

"We do!"

"Aye, yee may enter then."

Timmy followed Drump into the building. Timmy looked at the owner of the house who appeared to be a ruggedly handsome man. He had long, black hair with a maroon bandana circling his head. On the front of the bandana was a very cliché skull and bones. He had a thick ginger beard and a black eye patch covering his right eye. Some would say he looked like a pirate. The rest of his clothes would disagree, however. He wore a *Grease*-esque leather jacket with a 'Nirvana' t-shirt underneath. He also wore blue and yellow boardshorts with red flip flops topping the outfit off. Timmy noted that the inside of the house resembled the inside of a boat. Having never been in a boat, he had no frame of reference for this assumption.

"Thank you so much for letting us come in! We've had an awful day," said Timmy.

"Yee be welcome. I know what it be like to have a bad day. I have them every day," noted the pirate sombrely.

"What's your name?" asked Timmy.

"Me name? I be captain o' this here house. Captain Jack Sorrow!"

"So you're a pirate?"

"Aye, I be a pirate. I 'ave travelled the seven seas 'n plundered booty fer hundreds of years!"

"Hundreds? That's crazy! Did you know Blackbeard?"

"Aye, I knew 'um. Or at least I thought I knew 'um… I'd rather not talk about it!"

"Timmy go check out the house," said Drump. "Jack and I need to have a conversation."

"Sure."

Timmy started walking around the cabin, looking at the pirate's peculiar decorations. On the wall hung photos of a number of animals including horses and mice. The strange thing about these photos was that they seemed to be taken by the animals themselves. Timmy disregarded them as just very lifelike paintings. He saw the pirate's huge projector screen hanging from the ceiling. Below it was a press full of VHS tapes. Most notably he owned seasons one and two of the new hit T.V. show 'FRIENDS' and signed copies of Rocky I, II, III, and IV. Timmy saw the pirate's workout equipment, which was identical to what was used in the Rocky IV training montage. *'At least this will help us prepare for the Olympics,'* he thought. Just after that thought hit him, he looked up and saw four photographs of Circus Olympic winners on the wall. Underneath it was tens of gold, silver and bronze medals. *'A mighty amount of plunder... A true pirate,'* thought Timmy. Beside that was the pirate's journal. One page was already opened, so Timmy decided to look at the most recent entry:

'I miss him. Every day I wake up I forget he's gone and for that brief moment in time, I'm happy. That soon passes, and I feel the weight of the world crash down on top of me like a mighty wave no lifeboat could be saved from. I don't know what to do. I've travelled the four corners of the sea, yet somehow, I feel cornered.

On another note: I'm on season two of FRIENDS and I'm really digging this Ross character. He's got a monkey and now a son! Delighted for him. And honestly the guy has moxey. I'm giving the show five stars.'

Timmy stepped away from the journal and walked over to Drump. "I have to admit I was a little worried about your plan, but I feel very safe here now! He's very nice! Also, between me and you, he might be gay!"

"He? I think you mean she. And I'm pretty sure she's straight."

"No I'm talking about Jack Sorrow."

"Yeah. Jack is a woman."

"What?"

"Did she not tell you? To be fair, she's probably tired of explaining it to every person she meets. It's hard to explain how she ended up as a male pirate, but essentially, she has this… skill. It's almost like a superpower. At any moment she can literally transform into another person, another entity."

"I can't tell if you're being serious or not."

"I'm as serious as Steven!"

"Who's Steven?"

"Oh right… He's just this very serious clown I know. But anyway, I know her power is real because I've seen her do it before. Back when I was in Clown College, we were on a crazy night out and we ended up in the middle of nowhere. We had no way back to our dorm, so I decided to call her. And literally, before my eyes, she turned into a taxiwoman. I never found out how she got the power, but it's as magical as the Magician's illusions."

"A taxiwoman? As in she picked you up in her car?"

"Yes. Exactly!"

"Right…"

"But she spends most of her time as a pirate for some reason. She's been transforming and changing for years now, but I think she's settled on being a pirate."

"She said she's been a pirate for over 100 years."

"On and off, yes. But in between those years she's changed to many different people. Some of whom are literally fictional characters from T.V. shows she likes."

"Right…"

"You got a problem with that, Timmy?"

"No, no. It's just a bit strange is all."

"You know what else is strange?"

"What?

"I said 'you know what else is strange?'"

"Oh. What?"

"The way your mind works, Timmy, you bigot!"

The atmosphere went stale for a moment while the tension between them hung in the air.

"So… are we setting up camp here? Like training for the Circus Olympics."

"Looks like it. It's the safest place for us to be until we head to London. Jack and I are no strangers to competition, though. So, don't worry, you'll be in good hands. Jack actually introduced me to the Rocky series and for that I owe her my life. She also possesses certain 'enhancers' that may assist our training…"

"Like steroids?"

"Yes. But this stuff is the crème de la crème. Come Circus Olympic time you'll be even more jacked up than you could have ever imagined. You'll win gold. I have no doubt of that."

"That seems a bit unethical."

"It's allowed, don't worry!" said Drump checking over his shoulder with shifty eyes.

"If you say so," said Timmy. "So, where will I be sleeping?"

"I'll show you."

Timmy followed Drump up the stairs of the ship. He took Timmy into the second room on the right. Inside there was a double bed, a standing mirror, a window and little else.

"I need clothes…" said Timmy.

"I got you," said Drump as he took several clown outfits out of his sleeves. He handed them to Timmy, who placed them on the bed.

"Where did the Magician go?" asked Timmy.

"He was our offering. There's no way we could stay here without an offering, Timmy."

"An offering? Is she going to kill him?"

"Sort of. She's going to make him walk the plank."

"Jesus… Does the offering give her the powers? Or how does that work?"

"No. She just likes to make people walk the plank. Back in the day she used to do it at sea, but in recent decades she doesn't get the chance as often. So, she'll let you stay for as long as you like once you keep her happy."

"That's crazy. And we're not on a real boat. How is she going to make him walk the plank?"

"The moat, Timmy…"

"She's going to feed him to the clownfish?"

"Fucking hell, how many questions are you going to ask? There are three crocodiles in the moat as well, Timmy. Obviously. How would you expect a bunch of clownfish to protect the house?"

"I don't know… Can I watch the plank walking?"

"Sure. She's doing it starboard at the moment. That's starboard! Not port!"

Timmy made his way to the top of ship. He saw Jack and the Magician at the other side of the ship, beside the plank. The Magician's hands were tied behind his back with rope. His hat had been removed to avoid any potential rabbit interference.

"Walk th' plank now! Me crocs' bellies be munching for a crunching!"

"This is obscene! Let me go and I'll tell you everything you want to know about the Magicians! I'll tell you how they found you. I'll tell you how to know whether or not you're in an illusion!"

"And what use would that information be to me crocs? YAR HAR HAR! Now walk th' plank!"

"Please! I beg of you! Let me live! I thought I read that pirates didn't even like killing their prisoners?"

Jack ignored the Magician as she continued to poke him in the back with a toy pirate sword.

"Any last words?"

"None of this even matters," cried the Magician. Jack shrugged.

"It does to me crocs," she said before pushing the Magician over the side into the moat. The screams of the Magician were soon faded out by the crunching of the crocodiles.

13: The Nightmare Before Christmas

<u>A Mime's Interpretive Dance</u>

**dances* (very well and very quietly)*

Timmy spent the next few weeks training with Jack and Drump in Jack's ship to get himself ready for the Circus Olympics. With the help of a Rocky themed training montage and a dangerous number of needles injected into his ass, Timmy was on his way to being competition ready. Drump was a big fan of the Rocky film franchise and refused to help Timmy if it wasn't in the same way Mickey Goldmill helped Rocky Balboa. In Drump's mind Timmy was the perfect 'Rocky' – he was an underdog, a lot of people wouldn't give him a chance and also, he occasionally slurs his words.

After another good session of log lifting and snow running, Timmy headed for his bedroom. He whipped out some needles and stabbed his ass with his nightly dose of the big man juice. The training and juicing had been going on for months now and they were slowly approaching Christmas time. He placed the needles back into his side drawer, ticked off December 14th on his bedside calendar and took out his bedtime book: 'Snoozey Stories for Sleepy Clowns'. He opened the book and read the first line of that night's new story:

'Once upon a time there was a clown called-'

With that Timmy fell fast asleep.

Three hours later he woke up to the sound of knocking on glass. At first, he thought it was the window. He hopped out of bed and crept over to the window to see what sort of prank Drump or Jack was playing on him. He looked out through the window to see the moonlit garden that lay in front. There was nothing in sight. *'Maybe the noise was from a dream,'* thought Timmy. He took one last glance out the window before closing the blinds, shutting out the light of the full moon. He enclosed himself in complete darkness, with only the sound of his racing, terrified thoughts. He knew it would be difficult to get back to sleep but jumped back into bed nonetheless. He closed his eyes and started counting clown sheep.

Knock Knock

This knocking sound wasn't coming from the window. It was coming from the windowless wall on the opposite side of the room. Timmy lit the bedside lantern and jerked his eyes to the wall. All that stood before him was a full-length standing mirror.

Knock Knock

Timmy heard the noise come from the mirror this time. Unsure of how to react, he slowly pulled himself out of the bed, hesitantly making his way towards the mirror, wondering if he was still dreaming. He reached the mirror with the lantern in hand. Standing in front of the mirror, Timmy gazed into his reflection's eyes. He raised his right arm. The reflection followed. He raised his left arm. The reflection followed. Timmy shook his head thinking, *'What am I doing?'* He yawned and turned away, heading back for his bed. His reflection stood dead still.

Knock Knock

Timmy jumped and turned back towards the mirror. His reflection looked back at him, staring directly into his eyes. Timmy gazed back into his reflection's soulless eyes. He took a deep breath and raised his right arm once again. The reflection shook its head. The reflection motioned its hand to invite him in. Timmy's stomach curled.

"You want me to walk into the mirror?" whispered Timmy. The reflection nodded.

"I'm not going to walk into a mirror," assured Timmy as he gave his reflection a dismissive look.

"Are you sure? Your father is here..." coaxed the reflection in a deep, brisk voice. His voice echoed through the mirror and met Timmy's ears, sending shivers down his spine.

"No, he's not. This isn't real, I'm not falling for it," said Timmy as he went to turn away.

"Hybrid is here..." Timmy froze. Without saying a word, he walked toward the mirror. *'This is definitely a dream'* he thought. He walked headfirst into the mirror and smacked his face off the surface.

"PRANKED! Try again."

Timmy shook the embarrassment off himself and walked into the mirror. As he passed through, he felt a rush of blood to his head. The space around him inverted before his eyes; the ceiling turned to floor and the floor to ceiling. He felt lightheaded and forced his eyes shut for a few seconds.

When he opened his eyes, the whole room seemed to be reversed. The windowless wall was now on the opposite side of the room, as was the door and bed.

"What the fuck?" mumbled Timmy as he nervously looked around the room. His line of sight was coated in black and white and a hint of grey. It was as though he was wearing a dogeye lens (The dog equivalent of a fisheye lens).

Timmy looked around the miscoloured room, barely able to close his mouth from the shock.

"Where are they? You said they were here!" he shouted.

"I didn't mean 'here' as in right here. I meant here as in this side of the mirror."

"Well, where are they?"

"On this side of the mirror… Are you even listening?"

"I know that now! I mean where on this side of the mirror? Take me to them."

"Okay," echoed the reflection as he reached his hand out for Timmy to grab. Timmy moved his hand into the reflection's, but it just passed straight through, "Oh shit that's right, I'm a ghost," mumbled the reflection.

Timmy followed his ghostly reflection out of Jack's lovely house and into the nearby woods. The sky was charcoal black with the moon as white as a perfect pearl. The trees stood 20 feet high and were as grey and dull as these descriptions. Timmy's feet splashed through the unusually damp mud, drenching his pyjama bottoms. His reflection's feet did not, because he was a ghost.

"You're looking well anyways!" said the ghost, trying to release the tension.

"Thanks, and yourself!" replied Timmy.

They stopped walking as they reached a 100-foot lifeless, gloomy tree. At the bottom of the tree was an unwelcoming entrance to some sort of cave. Timmy's reflection insisted his father and Hybrid were at the end of this menacing cave.

"Your father and Hybrid are at the end of this menacing cave, I insist!" said the reflection.

"Are you not coming with me?"

Clownbound

"Sorry, but you're on your own now. I have ghostly activities and shenanigans to attend to."

Timmy reluctantly followed his heart into the cave. Water dripped from the cave's stony ceiling, splashing onto the rough, muddy ground. As he delved deeper into the cave the light became increasingly scarce. He eventually reached what seemed to be the centre of this underground structure. The space was dimly lit by torches on the walls.

Timmy stood against the wall when suddenly the light went out. Pitch dark. He couldn't see anything.

"What just happened?" asked Timmy. "Is somebody there?"

This was followed by silence. Absolute silence. Timmy could hear his own breathing become faster and faster as the time slowly passed. He couldn't hear or see anything, but he felt like he wasn't alone. The silence was slaughtered by a dull thumping echo in the cave.

He could hear the "splash… drip… drip… drip… splash…" as if whatever was moving was putting one foot in front of the other, real slow, like it was trying to be quiet. Fear clogged his throat. His pulse pounded in his ears. Timmy heard an unintelligible sound not too far from where he stood.

"Timmy… Come with me…" announced an unfamiliar, mechanical voice.

Droplets of sweat fell from Timmy's forehead as his hands started to tremble, "Ah here, fuck this!" shouted Timmy. He swiftly turned around and ran for the exit. He leapt out of the cave and back into the poorly lit forest.

The forest was shrouded in a white mist, making it very easy to see anything that was black or grey. Through the mist appeared an amorphous creature with two legs. Its entire body was jet black, making it difficult for Timmy to imagine what it could possibly be. As Timmy manoeuvred through the trees the clouds thickened, blocking out the light of the moon. The mist thickened. He looked over his shoulder and could see the creature following him at a slow, creepy, robotic speed. He picked up the pace and ran back to the ship. He made his way up the inverted, grey stairs and into the room he came from. As he stood in front of the mirror, he heard the front door swing open. A voice flew through the house and reached Timmy's ears,

"Bing Bop."

'What the fuck is going on?' thought Timmy as he jumped back through the mirror. He landed back in his normal room. He was disoriented as his brain tried to familiarise itself with reality. Timmy was still panic-stricken and knocked over the lantern on his way back to the bed. The smashing noise was soon followed by his bedroom door swinging open. Timmy screamed.

"Will you shut up? Seriously, shut the FUCK up!" roared Jack in her pink nightgown. "I was havin' a marvellous dream and you went and ruined it. I briefly felt the warmth of happiness for a moment and then you woke me up from me slumber and reminded me of me life. Thanks for that! Now just shut up and go back to your bunk or you can go join your friend with the crocs!" With that, Jack slammed the door shut. Timmy got back into bed and cosied himself under the covers. He woke up the next morning and assumed everything that happened before the lantern smashing was a dream.

24/12/1996 – PERU

After nine hours of vigorous training, Timmy, Drump and Jack made their way back inside. Inside the ship, the panting of Timmy echoed through all the rooms. His nose and ears were numb with the cold. He bent over, pushing his hands into his thighs so as not to fall over. Drump and Jack were in front of him. They were concerned that he was not ready for the challenge that lay ahead of him. His fatigue was painfully obvious, and another day's training could just about kill him. Timmy raised his head, crinkling the back of his neck and panting with his tongue out like a dog.

"Do you guys still think I got a shot at this?" said Timmy in search of encouragement.

"Not like this you don't!" shouted Jack, who then reached into her back pocket and pulled out three different needles. All three were different, luminous colours, looking like a miniature rainbow of green, blue and purple. With the three of them clenched in Jack's hand, she went right around Timmy and stabbed them into the left cheek of his ass simultaneously. The syringes pierced right through the shorts Timmy was wearing and when the syringe was pressed down Timmy screamed, 'AH HOY HOY CAPTAIN!'

Jack took a step back. She shared a concerned look and a shrug with Drump. However, this awkwardness soon passed as Timmy re-enacted the iconic scene in Rocky when he's majestically air punching at the top of a long stair case. This small act brought hope to the committed trainers and the clown world as we know it.

Clownbound

At last it was Christmas, what a wonderful sight,
Timmy got a day off before the big fight.

The crew rested in bed, all snuggled and warm,
Dreaming of Rocky and his boxing form.

Although whilst they lay tucked in bed, something was coming,
Santa, his reindeers, and his fat fingers numbing.

Mistletoe hanging, held breath, anticipation,
But what really would come, would shake the clown nation.

With a gaze cast skywards, the stars were glimmering,
But deep below the night sky, a danger was simmering.

Footsteps on the roof, they clicked, and they clacked,
Eyes were shut tightly, hoping stockings would be packed.

Sounds, they were roaring, not santa's roof-hopper,
But no, it was worse, a military chopper!

Saint nick slides down the chimney, late he is not,
But now clambers through windows, 3am on the dot!

Timmy lay up, til he could lay up no more,
He drifted to sleep, his eyes they were sore.

Eyes nailed tight and knuckles tightened more,
Almost asleep, but was there more in store?

A burst through the door, who was that you might ask?
It was GG and the Magicians! Which made the reader gasp!

Clownbound

Timmy snapped up to see what had come to enter,
It was his dreaded sister, to halt his adventure!

Luckily for Timmy, his friends heard the whole thing,
And just like a flash, to the room they did spring.

To his rescue they came, and that is no lie!
Drump and Jack barged in with their fists held high.

"The Circus Olympic regulations state clear and true,
You may not harm him; he's a competitor to you!"

"Harm Timmy I will not! Who, me? That's a crime!
But THIS won't be competing come Olympic time!"

GG held a large sack, popped right over her shoulder.
Then dropped it down, as the voice in the sack told her...

The sack opened up, like a broken man at an AA meeting.
And out rolled a fat round man whose forehead was bleeding.

"Gee willikers! That's Santa!" Jack roared with a fright,
"Who will now deliver the presents to the children tonight?"

"Ha ha ha! Santa? Who him? No more,
We cut open his head and brainwashed him." GG swore.

'Brainwashed him? Brainwashed him? Surely you cannot!
Saint Nicholas is neutral in this Clown-Magician plot!

"Oh, you think so, but I will prove you wrong!
Santa, have at that boy as if you were King Kong!"

Clownbound

He banged on his chest, he did so with such strength,
The clowns feared Christmas had just come and went.

Santa fiercely approached, with fire and wrath,
Until Captain Jack stepped into his path.

Captain Jack held a magical power, my god it did work!
Like medusa she had turned Santa to stone, GG went berserk.

'Another plan foiled!' GG roared the walls to rubble,
And just like that, Timmy was fresh out of trouble.

'Leave Jack's lovely house and never come back!
For if you return, we WILL surely attack.'

From a threat like that, tingles traced down her spine,
'I'll see you at the games' and she left with that line.

Timmy sprang out of bed and sprinted across the room
'Xmas is over, is that safe to assume?'

'Of course not m'boy' Drump said with a kick,
I'll break him out with laughter, I'll fix him with a trick.

Drump jumped and Drump flipped, he knocked over vases,
To try and elucidate a few funny faces.

He juggled balls, he jumped, he danced, and he fell!
He also did some things that I'm not allowed to tell.

Not too long after, changes began to happen,
The stone was moving, from Drump's ceaseless yapping!

Clownbound

A smirk turned to a smile and a smile to a giggle!
It wasn't long 'til his big belly started to jiggle!

It was scarcely a minute, the old king was back,
Bewildered, confused, looking for a Christmas snack.

Cookies and milk were brought to get him in order.
He got into a panic, said "There's gonna be murder!"

He put his fingers in his mouth and whistled away,
Within seconds his reindeer were outside with his sleigh.

"Well boys and...Jack, I'd best be going.
If I stay any longer, it will have stopped snowing."

Within the blink of an eye, it was Christmas morning!
He'd sprinkled sand on their eyes, leaving them yawning.

Timmy, with a smile, hopped down the stairs.
Presents were everywhere, easing his cares.

However, much to his shock all his presents were the same
Except for a letter, 'Beat them in Santa's name!'

Right after the letter, Timmy checked his Christmas stocking,
It was chock full of steroids, soon his arteries he'd be
blocking!

"Timmy after last night we know we're all very tired,
But we have to leave now; they have this place wired!"

Timmy ran for his suitcase and packed it tight as he could,

Clownbound

He would need all the needles to win, oh yes he would.

A long journey ahead, not to hit the specifics,
But they were finally on track to the Circus Olympics.

<u>A Midget's Slam Poetry</u>

Small in height, big in heart,
We are the Midgets.

Low in size, high in hopes,
We are the Midgets.

Tiny in structure, huge in strategy,
We are the Midgets.

Below average measurements,
Above average commitment,
We are
The Midgets.

09/01/1997 - London

After a twelve-hour flight and a near tragic plane crash involving eels, they had finally arrived in London. The clowns were said to have a huge home advantage in this Circus Olympics, seeing as England is full of clowns. The Circus Olympic village was disguised as Buckingham Palace, while the real Buckingham Palace was stolen and temporarily relocated to Wales. The Circus Olympians were stationed on the east end of the village, while all other guests stayed in a hotel nearby. Timmy parted ways with Drump before going to meet his fellow clown contestants.

The accommodation was split into ten separate parts, one dedicated to each faction of the circus; the Clowns, the

Magicians, the Midgets, the Tightrope Walkers, the Men who Walk on Stilts, the Trapeze Artists, the Acrobats, the Lion Tamers, the Contortionists and the recently inducted faction of Chimpanzees. Timmy made his way over to the Clown Building, dodging the faeces that the Chimps were throwing his way.

The Clown Building was situated between the Chimp Building and the Lion Tamer Building. The facility was filled with all the things clowns love such as a dancefloor and glowsticks. Making his way past the clown rave, Timmy went to his room, which he was sharing with three other clowns. To his surprise he was greeted with tension and animosity by his fellow roommates.

"Prljav," spat one of the clowns as he left the room. One of the other clowns followed him, but the other one stayed.

"What was that about?" asked Timmy.

"Oh, don't mind him! He's a silly billy! It was Croatian for 'dirty'... We've heard about you and my friend is convinced that all non pure-blooded clowns are subclown. Biggest load of rubbish you've ever heard right?" said the clown.

"What does he mean 'non pure-blooded clowns'?" questioned Timmy.

"He comes from a rich clown heritage and has clown prejudice when it comes to clowns who aren't... Well whose parents weren't clowns. You catching what I'm throwing?"

"I have caught what has been thrown, but that's stupid! I'm as much clown as anyone else here... In the clown building that is," snapped Timmy.

"Ay oh ay, woah, you don't gotta tell me that my clown. Tell him, ha ha. Look, sorry for his lack of manners, Timmy. It's Timmy, right?" said the clown in a rather calm manner.

"Yeah, that's fair enough and yeah, that's my name," said Timmy. "What's your name?"

"The name's Billy… Silly Billy," said Silly Billy. "Are you heading out for the opening ceremony tonight? I heard it's going to be clowntastic!"

"Yeah, I guess I will," said Timmy, slightly angered by the use of the word clowntastic.

"Clowntacular!" replied Silly Billy.

After unpacking his clothes and syringes, Timmy planned to rendezvous with Drump and Jack over coffee. They were set to meet up at a quaint, niche, Jewish-owned coffeeshop called 'He Brews', not too far from the village. Waiting for Drump and Jack to arrive, he decided to order his coffee.

"Can I get an Americano, please," requested Timmy.

"Oy vey," sighed the old Jewish lady behind the counter. "What's with all these kids and their Americanos and Cappuccinos? Back in my day we just drank straight coffee. There was none of this meshuggeneh."

"Ha ha yeah…"

"Oi kid, don't sweat it! You're not as bad as the shmucks that come in here ordering their mochas and their whatnots," laughed the barista as she handed him his coffee. Timmy walked over to an empty table, curious as to why the lady wasn't taken aback by the fact that he was wearing clown clothes and makeup.

"HONK HONK!"

Drump and Jack had finally arrived.

"Sorry we're late, Timmy! We were sightseeing!" said Drump.

"Ah that's okay!" replied Timmy. "What were the sights like? I haven't had a chance to check the place out. Is England a nice place?"

"No."

Clownbound

Drump and Jack got their coffees and sat down at the table. Drump got an Americano, while Jack got an Espresso, the very drink she suspected Ross Gellar would drink.

"Hey, can we sit over there?" asked Jack, as she pointed to a nearby couch with two seats either side of it.

"Um, I guess so. But why?" asked Timmy.

"Oh no reason…" replied Jack with shifty eyes, clearly attempting to recreate a scene from 'FRIENDS'. Her affinity for the hit T.V show 'FRIENDS' grew as the days passed.

They moved over. Drump and Timmy sat at the couch while Jack sat on one of the seats with a big grin on her face. Timmy was enjoying the warm coffee when Drump stopped him and asked, "What events have you signed up for?"

"Sign up? What? I assumed I did all the events, no?"

"HA HA, all of the events?? You fool. You think we'd send you into the pole vault against the Men on Stilts? You wouldn't stand a chance. That's a job for the tallest clown, Mr. Tall Clown!" spat Drump.

"Oh yeah," said Timmy, "I forgot about him... Well how many events can I sign up for?"

'Only three, so choose carefully," replied Drump. "Here's the list of events,' Drump handed him a folder consisting of several hundred pages. After scanning over all of them very quickly, Timmy decided on what events he wanted to participate in.

"Okay, I've made my mind up. I'll do the pie throwing event, the boxing, and the freestyle wrestling!"

"Are you sure you want to do the wrestling?" said Drump, worriedly. "Those chimps will rip you to shreds! What makes you think you could take on a chimpanzee when you couldn't even slap the head off Saint Nicholas?"

"Well what should I do instead?" asked Timmy.

Clownbound

"I think you're ready for the circuit race," said Drump with pride. He stood up. "This is the main event. All competitors hop on a unicycle and race to the death. Figuratively. They actually race to the finish line, but it's all very intense. Only the most remarkable clowns have been chosen to represent us in the circuit race and I think it's time you do too!"

"Wow... I would be absolutely honoured," said Timmy with a tear in his eye. "How does the Circuit work?"
"You begin with a 10km cycle on the unicycle. After this you must swim 20km. Once the swimming is done, you run back around the water and collect the unicycle you left behind. After that you skedaddle to the finish line for 50km on the unicycle. All in all, it should take about 15 minutes if you're decent."

Timmy made his way back to the village and handed in his form before the opening ceremony began. He went back to his room, where he was met by Silly Billy.

"Yo Timmy, good timing. We're about to head out to the ceremony. You coming with?" asked Silly Billy.

"Yeah sure!" said Timmy as he threw on his clown jacket and followed them out the door.

"Hey Silly Billy, do those guys still hate me?"

"Don't worry about them, Timmy. They'll come around. They always do," said Silly Billy.

The two clowns headed for the ceremony. The Circus Olympics' opening ceremony was a momentous occasion. Every year the faction with the most gold medals from the previous Circus Olympics had to perform some sort of entertainment for the opening ceremony, however, seeing as it was the Chimpanzees first year in the modern Circus Olympics, they had the honour of performing tonight. The arena seated 80000 people, just enough to fit all the Circus

Olympics contestants. Timmy and Silly Billy were a little late, so they had to sit in the Midget end of the audience. This was to their benefit because they had absolutely no trouble seeing in front of them.

"Sorry, I think you dropped this," said Timmy to the man in front as he went to hand him his fallen wallet.

"You talking to me?" asked Silly Billy.

"No, I was talking to the dwarf in front of us," said Timmy.

"What the fuck did you just call me?" asked the man as he turned around. "Did you just call me a fucking dwarf?"

"Wait, sorry, I thought that was the correct term. I didn't mean anything by it."

"I am a Midget, not a dwarf. We are the Midgets, not the dwarves, you absolute bigot."

"Okay, sorry. I won't make that mistake again," said Timmy as he handed the Midget his wallet.

"You're goddamn right you won't," spat the Midget as he grabbed the wallet from Timmy.

Everybody was very excited, because every Circus Olympic opening ceremony is always a tremendous show. The opening ceremony of the previous Olympics was hosted by the Magicians. They put on an incredible show with amazing magic tricks that still baffle most of those who saw it to this day. Even the clowns were impressed, particularly when the Magicians recreated the northern lights in three dimensions within the arena, before pulling a rabbit out of a hat. Many left that ceremony with tears from the beauty and those who witnessed it had high hopes for this year.

"SHHH!"

The chimps began to enter the arena. Everybody sat forward as they waited to see the show begin. Except, it didn't. The chimps just stood around playing with themselves. A number of the chimps just sat down making noises. The audience were divided. Half were disgusted, as they were expecting a tremendous show. The other half love the zoo, so were delighted to see these chimps monkeying around. This went on for three hours. Everybody had to stay and watch as it is forbidden to leave a Circus Olympic ceremony for any reason. Eventually the show ended, and the chimps were taken off stage. The audience applauded, more excited about the fact that it was finally over.

"I'm not sure why we expected anything else," sighed Silly Billy.

Timmy faked a nod, while really thinking, '*That was brilliant. I bloody love monkeys.*'

16: Let the Games Begin

The opening day of the 1997 Circus Olympics was finally under way, and the contestants couldn't have been more hyped up. Tension between the factions grew from casual competitiveness to all-out war. The eleventh faction of the Circus, the Mimes, were responsible for policing during the Circus Olympics. They wanted to participate in the events with all the other factions, but nobody would hear them out. Instead, they were on security duty and this year they had a big task set out for them.

Hooligans from all factions were chancing their luck and trying to cause a disruption on the opening day. Half were doing so to increase their faction's chances of winning while the other half were in it for the fame. Four Contortionist hooligans tried to stir up controversy by placing banana peels at random locations around the Olympic Village in the hopes that opposing competitors would slip and injure themselves. However, this is not what happened. Instead, the Chimpanzees found and gathered all the banana peels. When they discovered that these peels were banana-less they were furious. They hunted down the four perpetrators and captured them. Taking them into the back of their building, they held them hostage only to be returned in exchange for one hundred real bananas.

"They're bluffing!" insisted the Contortionist Chief Captain. However, after being sent a dismembered leg and three fingers they submitted and sent the Chimpanzees one hundred bananas. The Mimes tried their best to prevent this from happening but ultimately their voices went unheard.

Drama was a regular occurrence during every Circus Olympics. The only two factions that made an attempt to avoid these shenanigans were the Clowns and the Lion Tamers. This is the very reason why they won more often than not. Their eyes were always on the prize. The same cannot be said for the other factions, the Magicians in particular. This year the Magicians' victims appeared to be the Midgets. They designed propaganda posters and littered the Olympic Village with them. Hundreds of posters saying, 'Height Matters' and 'I'm Going to Kill All of the Midgets' covered the walls of the village. They robbed a theme park height restriction cut-out and wrote 'You must be this tall to be in the Circus Olympics' all over it. This attack left the Midgets feeling demoralised and lower than usual, but the Magicians didn't stop there. Following this, several Magicians snuck into the Midgets' building and moved all of their food and training equipment onto the top shelves. The Magicians involved were taken into Mime custody following the death of eight of the Midget athletes due to starvation. They were to be held in a big invisible glass block of the mimes' making for the remainder of the competition.

Following tradition, the first game that would be played would be the pie throwing competition. Timmy was nervous about this one. He felt himself getting cold feet. Maybe he wasn't ready, or maybe it was because his shoes didn't fit. Nonetheless he clowned up and attended the draw. Timmy was selected last to step up to the plate. The pie throwing competition had always been the first event of every Circus Olympics given how iconic of a gag it is. The event allows the pie throwing contestant to take a maximum 5-yard run-up. If the contestant takes any more steps or steps over the painted line, then they are disqualified from the entire tournament. The contestant must throw the pie high and forward. He or she must then run after the pie and try to land it on their own face. The effectiveness of the throw is measured from the point where the individual's last step is to the point where the pie connects with the face, multiplied by how centrally the pie lands on their face. 10 points are given for 100% accuracy and 1 point for a miss.

Timmy met up with his coaches, Drump and Jack, for a pep talk.

"This is the first event, Timmy. Are you excited?"

"Absolutely! But I'm also nervous. What if I mess up?"

"Come here, Timmy." said Drump. As Timmy walked to him, Drump slapped him across the face. "Mess up? You're a clown, Timmy! Throwing pies is our speciality. It's what we do. You'll do fine. I don't think a clown has ever lost the pie throwing event."

"Well, that just makes me more nervous now. What if I'm the first?"

"Timmy… these negative thoughts aren't going to get you anywhere! You're going to do fine. All you have to do is make it into the last 10 out of 30, which is easy. 3 competitors of each faction compete in each event. The Stilted Men never get further than 3 metres before their stilts lose balance. The Tightrope Walkers are too focused on balance to get enough distance. The Chimps will likely just eat their pies. This will be easy, don't worry about it."

"I guess so…"

Timmy watched the first two contestants enter the 'Pablo Piecaso Pietradome' and wished them good luck. He sat on a bench by himself, slouching over his shoulder, his feet tapping like he was part of a Riverdance. He was biting his finger nails like they were corn on the cob.

First up were the Lion Tamers. The Lion Tamers have always been a proud faction. Filled with courage and heart, they tamed lions for eons, helping mankind better understand the relationship between human and animal. Their flag, a yellow background with a glorious lion on the front, was first designed in the late 1700s. The lion on the front, Roy, encapsulates everything the Lion Tamers believe in; he was courageous, strong and warm-hearted. Many believe Roy to be a myth. Others are certain of the tale's truth. What they all agree on, however, is that Roy epitomises the perfect feline friend.

Timmy watched nervously, unsure of how they would do. The first Lion Tamer representative gave Timmy a thumbs up and a smile that stretched so wide it could have made Stretch Armstrong himself say, 'You stretched that smile very far.' A series of goosebumps travelled down Timmy's arms and up his back when the whistle blew. The Lion Tamer hurled his pie into the air. There was such might behind the throw that Timmy began to worry. He looked at Drump, who seemed surprised by the distance the Lion Tamer got. The pie landed back down on the smiling Lion Tamer's face. The Lion Tamer fans went crazy as it was revealed to be a world record. However, the steward asked for the replay to be shown on the big screen. At a second glance everyone realised his foot stepped over the line. This was one line that couldn't be tamed.

Timmy walked over to the bench of the Lion Tamer to offer his condolences and support to the newly disqualified competitor. Before he could speak, he saw his sister running over to him.

"HA HA HA! I guess that was the line you couldn't tame!" said Gabby, unknowingly stealing the narrator's joke and twisting it to sound mean when it was meant to be witty.

Timmy watched as the shape of the Lion Tamer's face seemed to crumble into itself. His tears fuelled Timmy with anger toward his sister.

Clownbound

"Unlucky pal," said Timmy, trying to encourage the disqualified competitor. He had read enough Spiderman comics to know that he can't let his anger get the best of him. "With great power comes great responsibility," he said to himself before pretending to shoot a web from his rock star shaped hand.

Timmy kept to himself, privately building up confidence for his turn. He knew if he continued to watch Gabby insult and undermine the failing competitors, he would only get angrier. Like the Incredible Thing from the Fantastic Avengers, he had to control his anger too or else it would ruin him. Finally, Timmy's head perked up like a deer hearing a gun shot. His name had been called out and his eyes lit up like there were two Human Torches in his head. He could hear Gabby shout abuse from across the field of play. The closer he got to the pie the louder she got, saying things like, "You are shite!" and "He's not going to throw that pie very far, ha ha." Timmy looked down at the pie, then looked up to the clowns in the Mime stand and said, "Don't worry, I hear you." The Magicians purposely forced the clowns to sit with the Mimes, so they wouldn't be able to make as much noise.

Timmy took a big deep breath and squatted down to pick up the pie. When he rose back up, the noise was no more. It was as if he had joined the clowns in the Mime stand. He was truly one of them. He looked over at his sister, now standing and screaming with spit flying out of her mouth. Her hatred could be heard no more. When he looked away from her and looked down the field of fallen pies, she was non-existent to him as if she was the Nonvisible Woman from the Fantastic Avengers.

Timmy heard the whistle from behind him. He looked up to the big screen to see the word "GO!" cover the screen, before changing to a shot of a child in the audience doing the

Running Man. Very well executed. Timmy lobbed the pie into the air and started running. He was well behind the line when he started his sprint. He closed his eyes and leapt forward as he prayed to the Clown Gods that he had timed it correctly.

SPLAT.

17: Now That's What I Call the Next Event at the Circus Olympics!

<u>A Lion Tamer's Poem - A Poem for Roy</u>

It was 1746,
In the African plain.

When I saw his face,
When I saw his mane.

With command he prowled,
He was difficult to tame.

Once domesticated, I loved him,
I know he felt the same.

He saved my life,
I named him Roy.

He died in 1758,
He was the goodest boy.

Timmy and the gang were delighted to find out that his pie throwing efforts had won him a spot in the next and final pie throwing event. After receiving this news, Timmy and his team headed back to the Clown House to celebrate. Everybody was hyped up from the performances at the pie throwing event.

"This is going to be such a wild night!" shouted one of the clowns. It was at this point Timmy knew he was in for a wild night. The clown that spat at Timmy started to cautiously walk towards him. He didn't know how to react. Should he see what he has to say, or should he slam him? He was stuck. The clown stood opposite him.

"Hey... Look I'm sorry for the way I treated you... I didn't know..." The clown stopped and took a deep breath. "I just didn't know you could throw a pie like that. There's no way you're anything but a clown with a throw like that."

"Thanks, it's fine…" Timmy turned away but immediately turned back. "Actually, you know what? It's not fine!"

"Whaaaaaaat?" said the other clown in a cartoony way, clearly taken aback.

"You heard me! You judged me before you knew me, and I cannot respect that! I cannot and I will not," roared Timmy at the top of his lungs. "Change your ways, clown, or I'll change them for you!"

The clown took a step back. "I…I'm sorry. You're so right, though. My negative vibes have only led me to a troublesome mindset. I need to embrace the positive vibes and not judge."

Timmy placed his hand on the clown's shoulder. "There you go, good clown. What's your name anyway, kid?"

"Klown," said Klown.

The clown party was about to get started so Silly Billy made his way up to the Disk Jockey.

"Yo DJ, play this shit," said Silly Billy as he handed the DJ his copy of '50 greatest songs in history, as voted for by clowns'.

"Ha ha, you got it, clown," replied the DJ with a wink. He put the record on shuffle and, off the bat, the 6th greatest song of all time, as voted for by the clowns, started to play.

"Let me hear you say 'Yeah!'
Let me hear you say 'Yeah!'

Clownbound

No no, no no no no, no no no no, no no there's no limit!"

This song was being played on repeat and when the time came, all the clowns would stop and sing:

"No no, no no no no, no no no no, no no there's no limit!"

Every clown immediately started getting down and moving like only a clown could move. They started throwing every shape imaginable: triangles, circles, even squares.

"This is my jam!" shouted eight different clowns at once. Timmy started letting loose for the first time in a long time.

"Woah Timmy, you got moves," said Silly Billy, who gathered a group of clowns that made a circle around Timmy. Timmy began to move like none of these clowns had seen before. Gasps filled the room as he threw in some dance moves that people didn't know existed at the time. Timmy did the robot for hours on end. For the first hour, the crowd were impressed. However, his second hour into doing the robot, the crowd got suspicious. Whispers of "No one could be THAT good at the robot." Newly arrived guests murmured, "You're telling me that's not a robot?" Timmy was on his third hour of doing the robot when everyone at the party grabbed some kind of weapon and organised how they were going to find out if this guy was a robot or not. A tense, stiff atmosphere took over the party. Timmy took no notice, but he was about to get trampled on. Suddenly, a man walking on stilts was walking backwards and shouting to his friend across the room carelessly with two drinks in his hands, "Chad I'll be fine for tomorrow! You know I can drink so many beers!" And just like that his stilts bumped into Timmy, spilling the drink all over Timmy, but Timmy just kept on roboting. The crowd were stunned to find out he wasn't a robot after all.

Clownbound

"God damn..." said Klown as he shook his head, laughing. "How did I ever doubt this guy?"

Timmy was being given free drinks by every second clown and, at this point in the night, he was incredibly tipsy. While taking another sip from his silly straw, he heard a voice behind him.

"Timmy, what are you doing?!"

He turned around to see Drump standing in front of him, as angry as somebody who went to the shop, picked out all their shopping and then realised they left their credit card at home.

"Woah ayy Drump, turn that frown upside down," joked Timmy, making fun of Drumps frowning lipstick.

"You have your first boxing match of the Circus Olympics tomorrow, Timmy! You need to be fresh, or you won't even last one round!"

"No no, no no no no, no no no no, no no there's no limit!"

"Ugh! Relax old man," stammered Timmy, falling over his hilariously long shoes.

"Good Clown, Timmy, you're a mess!" said Drump, clearly angered by Timmy's state.

"HA HA, did you see that HA HA. What a fall HA. I haven't fallen that hard since..." Timmy suddenly started crying.

"No no, no no no no, no no no no, no no there's no limit!"

Wiping tears from under his eyes, Timmy followed up, "Since I fell for her." At this point he couldn't hold it in. He was roaring crying and causing a scene.

"Timmy, it's okay, I'll take you to bed." Drump lifted him up and carried him to his bedroom.

The next thing Timmy could remember was waking up to the sound of his roommate humming

"No no, no no no no, no no no no, no no there's no limit!"

With a huge groan he pulled himself up in the bed. His head was pounding, and the room was spinning.

"Uggghh, what time is it?"

"Ayy look who's awake! Mr. Slick Dance Moves! You threw so many shapes last night that I thought we were playing Jenga!" laughed Klown.

"What the fuck does that even mean," snapped Timmy, visibly dehydrated. "Also, what time is it, clowndammit!? I don't have time for your clowning around!"

"8:35…" Klown's enthusiasm lowered. "Wait, don't you have your first fight today? What time's that at?"

"SHIT!" interrupted Timmy. "It's at 9! I gotta go!"

Timmy jumped out of bed and darted out the door, knocking over Klown and Silly Billy's unfinished game of Jenga.

Drump and Jack were eagerly waiting ringside. Drump was drinking his fifth cup of coffee of the day. His hand was shaking as he took another sip. Jack was noticeably less nervous. She was taking sips from her rum flask to calm her nerves.

"Where be he?" questioned Jack. "He better show up!"

"Damn right he better show up," said Drump. "We can't afford to lose the first round. If we do, the clowns will be the laughing stock of the Circus!"

Just as they were beginning to lose hope, they saw Timmy running towards them.

"I am SO sorry!" he cried, as he tried to catch his breath.

"It's okay Timmy, the fight isn't on yet!" said Drump. "I just hope you're ready."

"I am, I am... I just didn't get a chance to look at the fixtures yet. Who am I fighting? Also, do you have my gloves?"

"Daddy Long Legs, the number 1 boxer in the Men who Wear Stilts rankings. And don't make me laugh Timmy... gloves? We don't use gloves in the Circus Olympics. Bare-knuckle. Go hard or go home. Have you picked your boxing name yet?" replied Drump.

"Oh, that's pretty hardcore… and no I haven't. Maybe like 'Hands of Steel'? Something like that?"

"Well that's awful. I do have an idea for a name though! One of the greatest clown boxers of all time was 'Tim Tim' back in 1746. If you like that name, I'll give that over to the announcer!"

"Sounds good to me!" replied Timmy, running on the spot trying to warm himself up.

"The fight will commence in 10 minutes! Time for the walkouts ladies and gentlemen," announced the announcer.

"Alright, Timmy! Get ready! You'll be walking out second. We picked your walkout music so don't worry. Just focus and get the job done. All the hard work has been done, now comes the fun part!" shouted Drump, getting Timmy hyped up.

Daddy Long Legs started running towards the ring while the anthem of the Men who Wear Stilts played in the background.

'Uptown girl,
She's been living in her uptown world,

I bet she's never had a backstreet guy,
I bet her momma never told her why…'

The crowd went nuts. Daddy Long Legs was the best boxer the Stilted Men have had in centuries and his following included people outside the Men who Wear Stilts, which was unusual for any faction in the Circus.

"Here we go, Timmy. It's time."

Timmy started shadowboxing and moving towards the ring. His appearance was met with applause from the clowns. The song *Eye of the Tiger* started playing. "I'll be honest, Drump, I was expecting the 'No no' song to play," said Timmy with surprise.

"Oh yeah, that would have been pretty funny. A good callback. But then again, Timmy, I fucking love Rocky."

With both Timmy and Daddy Long Legs in the ring, the announcer began to introduce the fighters.

"And in the blue corner, fighting out of the Men with Stilts faction, with a record of 23-0, the 'HEIGHT OF PAIN', none other than Daddy LONG LEGS!"

The crowd erupted, cheering and chanting "Daddy! Daddy!"

"And in the RED corner! Fighting out of the clown faction, making his boxing debut! Timmy Tim Tim 'Tim Tim' THOMPSON!"

Timmy and Daddy Long Legs met in the centre of the ring with the referee holding them apart. The referee looked at Timmy.

"I expect a clean fight. You know the rules. Now touch hands and back to your corners!" The referee turned around to Daddy Long Legs, looking up at the towering man and his 6-foot-tall stilts.

Timmy headed back to his corner. Hopping on the spot, left foot facing straight ahead with his right foot behind angled to the right, he was ready. He moved his hands up, blocking his chin with his elbows in.

"FIGHT!"

Timmy rushed in. He could barely hear anything with the noise from the crowd. He threw a jab at Daddy Long Leg's left stilt, wobbling his balance. He followed this up with a right hook, snapping the left stilt entirely. Daddy Long Legs completely lost his balance on the one stilt, falling headfirst into the ring.

SPLAT

Drump and Jack jumped into the ring and lifted Timmy up.

"You did it, Timmy! Brilliant," shouted Drump.

"Wait, shit, is he okay?" asked Timmy, concerned for Daddy Long Legs.

"Look Timmy... if he died he died," replied Drump, delighted with himself for the inaccurate Rocky reference.

Minutes later, after getting over Daddy Long Legs' death, Timmy excitedly announced, "So I'm into the semis!"

"Did you not hear, Timmy? The chimpanzee tore his opponent to shreds and ate him in the ring, so he's been disqualified! You're into the final!!" said Drump.

"Wait what... But I killed Daddy Long Legs? Why am I not disqualified?"

"Because you did it by accident, didn't you?" said Drump with a strong wink.

"Oh okay… So, who am I facing in the final? And when is it?"

"Diego the Tight Rope Walker in four days! We'll need a different tactic. You won't be able to knock this guy off his balance. That's kind of his expertise."

"Ha ha true!" laughed Timmy.

Clownbound

"Now go home and get some rest. You have the boxing final at 10am tomorrow and the next round of pie throwing just after it. And don't forget we have the BIG circuit race next week!"

18: It's Reptime

Timmy woke up in a cold sweat at 4am the morning of his next event. He sat up in his bed, brushing back his hair while looking at all of his roommates. They were conked out asleep. He tried to fall back asleep, but it was no use. There was too much on his mind. The pressure was on. He was truly at the business end of things. *'What if the big day comes and we're fresh out of coffee.'* He began to sweat even more. Timmy wasn't addicted to coffee, he just had to have it every day or else he would have mood swings and wouldn't be able to function properly. If there was no coffee available on the day – even though he wasn't dependant on it at all – he would be in no shape to compete.

He knew he wasn't going to be able to sleep, so he jumped out of his bed and stretched. He put on his clown running shoes, grabbed a bottle of water from his bedside locker and snuck out of the dorm room. As he left the Clown House, he was hit with the shivering January British breeze. Goosebumps formed on his arms as his neck tightened. The smell of popcorn mixed with cigarettes hit Timmy's nose. He took in his surroundings as he walked through the Circus Olympic Village. He witnessed several contestants sneaking back into their buildings after coming from a forest rave. He continued to walk until he was in a quieter area of the village. Standing in the centre of the Circus Olympic Village, Timmy looked up to the stars and took a deep breath. Five years after he lost his family. Months after he lost the love of his life. Here he was. One night's sleep away from Circus gold. "I'm doing this for you, baby," said Timmy. He was aware that he hadn't properly mourned Hybrid and his fathers' deaths. He thought that winning gold might help, but he wasn't fully convinced. He stretched his calves and hamstrings and then started jogging. His size 17 clown runners smacked the ground vigorously with every stride he took. The cold breeze numbed his nose and ears as he ran past the silent faction buildings. Not a noise was to be heard as he ran by the Mime building, because, as we all know, Mimes go to sleep many hours before 4am.

As Timmy jogged, he noticed something behind him. He thought he was being followed. He turned right past two buildings and turned left through a set of trees to see if he was right. After hearing a whoosh sound, he glanced behind him to see that there was a shadowed figure not too far behind him, trying to blend in with the surroundings. His heart rate increased rapidly. He stood still to see if the figure approached him. It did. As the shadowed figure grew closer, Timmy knew he had no choice but to turn left and head toward one of the faction's buildings. He sprinted for the closest building to him. When he reached it, he tried to open the door. It was locked. He could hear talking from the inside.

"Well quite frankly, Charles, that is beyond your jurisdiction. Perhaps you should avoid overstepping your boundary and—" A chimpanzee glanced out through the window and saw Timmy banging on the door. He dropped his cigar and screamed, "HUMAN!!"

Timmy looked over his shoulder and saw the scaly predator coming in his direction. He stopped knocking and barged through the door shoulder first. The door flew off its hinges landing flat on the ground. Timmy continued running through the Chimpanzee House, occasionally looking behind him. He was so fixated on escaping that he didn't take in what was going on around him. The Chimpanzees were frantically trying to erase plans from their blackboards and hide their Chimpubian Cigars. They began screaming to intimidate

Timmy out of the building, but he was too worried about the entity following him to notice. After turning his head to get another look at what was following him, Timmy bumped into a chimpanzee with noise cancelling headphones on. The chimpanzee was hyping himself up for the big circuit race and couldn't hear a thing.

"Oi! What's this then?!" roared the chimpanzee as he took off his headphones. He turned around to see Timmy running. "Oh shit..." The chimp started hooting and banging his chest. He began smacking his hands off the floor as Timmy continued to run out through the side door and back into the village.

Once out of the building it seemed as though he had lost the reptile. He was now in an area of the Circus Olympic Village that he knew led to the exit. At the edge of the village stood a large house with four pillars in front. Timmy knew he would need to go through this building to get outside the village and to Drump and Jack for safety. The building was brick red with white pillars and arches. At the top of the building was three Greek letters that Timmy had never seen before. Music was being blared from every corner of the building. The closer he got to the building the louder the music got – a thumping techno bass vibrating through the air. When he reached the building, he saw the being swerve around the corner of the Chimpanzee House with malicious intent. Standing in a lit area, Timmy could see it was a lizard. Timmy knocked on the door of the building. The door was opened by a man with a pig mask on.

"Bro! Get the frick in here. We're partying down right now!" slurred the man with the pig mask. Timmy took one quick look behind him. The lizard was closing in.

"Fricking gnarly, brother," he said as he came into the house, slamming the door behind him.

Clownbound

Timmy made his way through the party. He grabbed a horse mask to try blend in with the party. He turned around as the strobe lights obstructed his vision. He saw the lizard get the same welcoming from the pig-masked man. He could see the lizard trying to blend in by throwing groovy moves and putting on a giraffe mask. This night was the Annual Animal Mask Party. Everybody on the dancefloor was wearing animal masks, making it difficult for Timmy to distinguish human from animal. Timmy was constantly seeing people with lizard masks as he made his way through the party. All around him were drunk Olympians who had already been knocked out of their events. Timmy saw the Lion Tamer who crossed the line in the pie throwing competition participating in other line related activities. He witnessed some of the Stilted Men toasting a drink to their fallen hero, Daddy Long Legs. What surprised Timmy the most was seeing Drump and Jack sitting on the couch chatting.

'What the fuck are they doing here?' thought Timmy. He came up behind them and called their names. They were too engrossed in their conversation to hear Timmy. However, he could hear them.

"I miss this! We used to talk all the time. What happened?" asked Drump.

"I don't know matey. I feel like since I became a pirate, I've just been up to me neck in barnacles, you know? But like sometimes I wasn't even busy. Me noggin was in the pits of Atlantis, you know? I blame meself!"

"Jack… Don't blame yourself. I'm as much to blame. But seriously, how are you these days?"

"I don't know matey… These last few moons have been weird. It doesn't feel… real? I don't know. Since we linked crews at me ship everything has felt… odd. This is probably just the rum talking."

"Bro… I totally get it. I totally understand. It's like th—"

Timmy slapped Drump in the back of the head. "Are you deaf?" roared Timmy. "I've been trying to get your attention and you two are just talking some pseudo-philosophical shite!"

"Jesus. First, sorry Timmy but it's very loud in here. Second, try that again and see what happens. Now what are you doing here? You've got an event tomorrow!"

"I'm being followed by a lizard!"

"A lizard? Shit. That's probably Pippens!"

"Pippens?"

"Diego's lizard. It's the night before your fight with Diego and suddenly a lizard is following you. Use your head, Timmy. Obviously, Diego sent his lizard to beat you before you even get to the ring."

"Well what are we going to do?"

"Get out me way ya swashbucklers! Leave it to me!" said Jack as she jumped off the seat. She was off balance and started laughing. "HAR HAR HAR. You guys have unlimited tissues up your sleeves, but I have a trick up mine, HAR HAR."

Jack ran out the door and Drump and Timmy just looked at each other. They played one game of beer pong before following her out the door. When they got outside, she was nowhere to be seen.

Timmy was relieved as he couldn't see the lizard, but before he could say, "wubbidy dubbidy Ryan Tubridy", the lizard reappeared and screeched as it pegged toward them.

"Quick, Timmy! Hop on this!" shouted Drump as he pulled out two unicycles from his pocket. Both Timmy and Drump rode the unicycles in the hopes of avoiding the reptile's grasp.

"Oh God no!" shouted Drump. Timmy looked over his shoulder to see Drump slowing down.

"What's wrong, Drump?"

"I have a burst tire! I need to change it, but there's no time. The lizard is right there!"

"We'll make time," said Timmy as he turned his unicycle back around. "Pass me the spare tire!"

Drump reached up his sleeve and pulled out a yellow rimmed unicycle tire. Drump got off the unicycle and handed it to Timmy. Timmy took a hammer out of his back pocket and unscrewed the tire from the wheel. He then hammered the new wheel onto the unicycle.

"Easy peasy squeezy lemon," said Timmy as he handed the unicycle to Drump.

The lizard was now back in sight as the two men rode the unicycles around the corner into an alleyway. As they turned the corner, they both jolted to a stop. In front of them stood a 10-foot-tall brick wall blocking their path. Timmy went to turn around, but the lizard had already reached the corner. A chime of snips echoed between the walls surrounding them. The lizard stood in front of them snipping a scissors with a clear sinister scheme planned.

"Good Clown! That lizard has a scissors!" screamed Timmy.

"This might be it…"

Suddenly, another lizard came from over the wall. Its body was stretched out, making it taller than Timmy or Drump. When it landed on all fours, it stood up on its back legs and began walking like a human. It walked over to Pippens and swung a left fist at Pippens' liver. Pippens dropped to the ground and got smacked with a kick to the head. Pippens managed to get back to his feet and tried to run away. In doing so, he tripped, cut his leg with the scissors, and knocked himself out on the concrete. He should have known not to run with scissors. The new lizard then stood over the unconscious, cut up body and spat on its forehead. Timmy buried his heels into the ground. He didn't know what was going on. He gulped. Hearing Timmy's gulp, the lizard turned around. As it turned around Drump saw its face and sighed.

"Phew! Am I glad to see you, Jack!"

"Told you I had you covered, boys!" said Jack as she winked one of her green eyes. "Now, I gotta go change back!" She then threw Pippens over her shoulder and pumped her legs rapidly, running on two feet into the distance.

"We sure got lucky, huh?" laughed Drump.

"What… the fuck…" said Timmy. "Jack literally turned into a human-sized lizard. How is that possible? That was the weirdest, scariest thing I've seen in my entire life. Was it even necessary? Like, why didn't she just hit him as a pirate? Why did she need to be a lizard to hit him?"

"I told you she could transform. You should have seen it when she transformed into a human-sized ant. THAT was terrifying!"

Timmy gazed aimlessly, still confused and shocked by what he had witnessed. "Where is she taking Pippens?"

"Don't worry about that, Timmy. We're just going to ask it a few questions," said Drump. He jumped back on his unicycle. "Now go back to bed and get some rest for tomorrow, Timmy!" Drump pedalled the unicycle and he was off like a hamster in a ball.

It was 5:30am when Timmy made his way back to his dorm room. He snuck back into his bed past his sleeping roommates. As soon as his head hit the pillow he conked out. He was woken up by his alarm at 7:30am. He sat up in the bed and noticed a letter taped to his pyjamas top. It read:

Clownbound

"Dear Timmy,

We stayed up all night 'negotiating' with that creature and the news we gathered was somewhat surprising. I'll break it down because I want to keep this simple.

- *Diego did in fact send Pippens to attack you.*
- *He sent his lizard to your room to cut off your hands, so you wouldn't be able to compete.*
- *Also, did you know Diego cried watching Mamma Mia!? Ha Ha crazy right?*

Anyways Drump and I are going to get a coffee to get our buzz on for today's training. YOU KNOW WHAT I'M TALKING ABOUT!

From Jack ☺ "

<u>A Tightrope Walker's Haiku</u>

We Tightrope Walkers:
If we fall, we are so boned,
Our job is risky!

Today was a big day for Timmy. He had his boxing final against Diego at 10am and the next round of the pie throwing event at 1pm. The potential for circus gold was within his grasp. He hopped out of bed with enthusiasm, waking his roommates, Silly Billy, Klown and the other clown. He was confused as to how they had managed to sleep through the events of last night yet were so easily woken up this morning. Klown made his way to the bathroom with a limp in his step.

"Why are you walking so awkwardly?" asked Timmy.

"I don't know, I've been like this for the past few weeks," admitted Klown with a sigh.

"Maybe it's your shoes?" interjected Silly Billy.

"Nah, I don't think that's it," said Klown.

"It might be!" announced the other clown, whose name has yet to be revealed, "I had a similar problem not so long ago and my orthopaedic doctor prescribed me these shoes for me. Try them on!" said the other clown as he handed Klown his spare shoes.

"I doubt it'll work, but I'll try." Klown placed his feet into the shoes and tied the laces tight. He stood up with a surprised look on his face.

"So, did they work?" asked Timmy.

"Yeah… I stand corrected!" said Klown in the orthopaedic shoes. He walked into the bathroom with a more comfortable stride.

Klown came out of the bathroom with his clown makeup on all ready to go.

"Hey Klown, I think you drew your eyebrows on too high," remarked Timmy.

Klown looked surprised.

"You also look miserable! We're clowns. We're supposed to be joyful and whimsical. As well as being the protectors of the people, of course," said Silly Billy.

"How do I make myself look friendlier then?" asked Klown, clearly agitated at the other clowns roasting him.

"How about you turn that dirty clown frown right upside down!" shouted the unnamed clown as he climbed into the cannon beside the window and launched himself across the Circus Olympic Village.

"What's got him in such a hurry?" asked Timmy.

"He has the next round of his pie throwing event later today, so he likes to get in as much practice as possible," replied Silly Billy as he got in his morning jumping jacks.

"Oh I'm in that event… I didn't realise clowns could compete against each other," admitted Timmy.

"Of course they do Timmy. Otherwise, there would only be ten in every event, you idiot. And sorry to say, but you have no chance against him! He's the best damn pie throwing clown I've ever seen."

Timmy didn't let this discourage him. He got ready for his big boxing final against Diego and headed for the ring.

Timmy arrived just in time and made his walk into the ring. Something felt a bit off. He had seen Diego's team beforehand and they did not look particularly confident. With the *Eye of the Tiger* dying down, Timmy stood in the corner of the ring, shadowboxing, ready to go. Across the ring Timmy could see Jack and Drump licking their lips. Through his lip-reading skills, he was just about able to make out what they were saying.

"YUMMY, that wizard stew was delicious last night!"

'Wizard stew? When did the guys get wizard stew? And what is wizard stew?' Timmy thought to himself.

With *'Jailhouse Rock'* blaring through the speakers, Diego slumped into the ring. He had noticeably poor posture and an aura of defeat. Tears rolled down his cheeks as he tilted his head to face the ground. *'Why is Diego so sad?'* Timmy thought to himself. None of this was making any sense to him. Diego wasted no time and walked straight up to Timmy and said,

"Did you kill my Pippens? Why would you do that to me? WHY?"

Timmy took a step back and gasped, "What!? I didn't kill your lizard. He's alive! He tried to catch these hands yesterday, but we got the bastard and interrogated him... but we did NOT kill him. I promise you that!"

"Oh yeah? Then what's this?!" Diego handed Timmy a letter. It read:

'Dear Diego,
We ate your lizard. We made him into a big lizard stew and ate him. That's what you get for messing with the gang!'

Timmy noticed that the bottom of the letter remained unopened. "This bit hasn't been opened yet," said Timmy.

"What?" gasped Diego as he grabbed the letter from Timmy's grasp. Diego opened the crease at the bottom of the letter. Diego's eyes followed the words before his face turned pale. His body went limp, as he fainted to the floor. The referee ran over and began counting from 1. Timmy picked up the piece of paper and read it.

'P.S.
Your lizard screamed the whole time. He tasted like well-seasoned lamb. Sorry we had to send you this letter, we didn't have the chops to tell you in person. Our baaad. See you in a while, Crocodile.

☺ Jack.'

"9… 10, its over, its over!" announced the referee as he waved his hands around Diego's body.

'Wow…' Timmy thought to himself. *'I can't believe Jack is getting so much use from the letter maker I bought him… It was meant to be a joke present.'*

Drump and Jack jumped into the ring, oozing with enthusiasm.

"You did it, Timmy! You won gold! You beat the almighty Diego!! How does it feel?"

"It's a weird feeling. I mean I didn't do much. I literally threw two punches throughout whole competition…" Timmy humbly noted.

"Yes, but wow what great punches they were," said Jack as Drump looked at Timmy and mouthed, "Wow."

"So is that it then? I'm a gold medallist clown?" asked Timmy. "That was easy."

"Yes you are, but don't let that go to your head Timmy. Your ego is kind of bothering me right now," asserted Drump. Jack nodded in agreement. "You still have a big pie throwing event in an hour, so try to humble yourself before that Timmy, yeah?"

"Okay… I was just…"

Drump interrupted Timmy, "Look nobody likes a show-off Timmy okay? And if anything, you only won because we whooped you into shape, juiced you up on 'roids and ate that delicious lizard."

"That is true," agreed Jack.

"Okay... I'll see you guys at the pie throwing event," said Timmy nervously. He walked towards the dressing room but could hear Drump in the distance.

"Don't get me wrong Jack, I love Timmy, but the fucking lip on that kid sometimes."

"You're telling me! HAR HAR" laughed Jack as they fist bumped and disappeared into the distance.

Timmy arrived at the pie throwing event with some time to spare. He stretched his pie throwing limbs and began practicing with the practice pies. These practice pies were made of marble and the practice area allowed you to throw them at marble statues. The reason for this was because the circus janitors refused to clean any more pie mess than necessary but had absolutely no problem cleaning marble off the floor. When asked why, the janitors would always say, "Who am I? The bus man?" undoubtedly an inside joke amongst the janitors. These circus janitors were as lazy as Irish politicians and as incompetent as Irish politicians. They didn't dress up as clowns or magicians, yet their uniforms made them look like the silliest individuals in the whole Circus Olympics. Wearing grey t-shirts and black workman trousers, these poor people would get abuse every time a contestant walked past. Timmy was no exception.

"Get out of my way, greyshirt!" demanded Timmy as he barged through two Circus janitors. This behaviour seemed out of character for Timmy, but it happened, so I don't know what to tell you.

"Scum, aren't they?" remarked Timmy's roommate as he spat at the janitors.

"Ha ha they sure are," laughed Timmy as he shook the clown's hand. "Are you ready for this event?"

"Born ready, Timmy! No offence, but I kind of have this in the bag…"

"I don't know about that! I'm pretty sure I'll give you a run for your money," Timmy playfully replied.

"Not a fucking chance. Your pie throwing skills are pathetic in comparison to me. No offence, but even using your name in the same sentence as mine and pie throwing is insulting to me and what I have achieved," said the nameless clown.

"We'll see about that!" Timmy said with competitive venom.

However, the nameless clown was right. Timmy finished fifth, while the other clown finished 1st by approximately 5 pies. Timmy walked up to the other clown with an offer of congratulations.

"Congratulations!" he said.

"Thank you, Timmy!" replied the other clown. "I'll be honest, you did better than I expected. You've earned my respect." This newly earned respect put a smile on Timmy's face. The other clown went to walk away towards the horizon when Timmy shouted towards him,

"Wait! What's your name?"

The clown stopped and turned his head towards Timmy with a cheesy grin. He then turned back around without speaking a word. The mystery of that particular clown's name continued.

Drump and Jack arrived shortly after.

"Well hopefully this has humbled you Timmy! If I'm being honest, I think you needed this loss before the big circuit race. You were getting a bit big for your boots… and these are some **BIG** boots we wear!" said Drump.

"You're probably right! Anyway, I'm ready to get to work for this big circuit race now!"

"Easy there, Timmy!" said Jack as she placed her hand on Timmy's shoulder. "The mighty dash isn't fer another week! Tonight, ye should go t' the Mid-Olympics Gathering in the Magician's house with yer roommates! That'd be a good wind down, and then we can get back t' work!"

"Sounds good to me!" said Timmy as he removed Jack's hand from his shoulder.

Timmy arrived at the gathering with Silly Billy and Klown. The place was packed to the brim, much like a modern local circus. The clowns grabbed some drinks and sat over by the concrete balcony.

Timmy, peered over the rusty nail barrier and scanned the room, looking at all the famous faces. He could see the controversial new circus rapper, Lil Salmon, from the Midget faction, talking to the Men with Stilts faction's very own Yao Ming. In the distance he could see someone he didn't recognise.

"Who is that?" asked Timmy, pointing to a clown doing the robot dance to perfection.

"That's 'Bing Bop', the first Robot Clown," replied Silly Billy. Silly Billy pulled Timmy in closer and whispered, "He doesn't know he's a robot, though, Timmy. We can't let him know. If he finds out that we've all been lying to him this whole time, we're doomed. He has the capability to blow up a whole country with the click of his fingers. He just doesn't know it yet."

Timmy took a step back. "That sounds dangerous."

"Oh he's dangerous alright. He might be the greatest weapon mankind has ever known."

"Okay but why is he moving his hand like that?"

"Like what?"

"Like that... Look at this hand." Timmy pointed toward Bing Bop, who was flamboyantly flopping his hand down.

"Ehh Timmy, he's gay."

"What? He's a robot."

"And?"

"Why was he programmed to be gay?"

"Ehm, why not?"

"Because he's a robot? Why would they specifically choose to make him gay?"

"What are you trying to say?"

"Were they trying to make a point? And if so, what point? I don't get it..."

Silly Billy scoffed, "Ehm, excuse me, Timmy? Why would they have programmed him to be straight? What difference does it make?"

"But why programme him to..." Timmy hesitated. "Never mind, I don't want this to become a whole thing."

"Wow okay. I know you're from Eastern Europe, Timmy, but I NEVER expected you to be homophobic."

"I'm n... Let's forget about it."

"Can't. I never forget a bigot. But if you speak to him just know that he's programmed to make a weird noise at the beginning of every sentence. Don't bring any attention to it, just ignore it."

"Okay I won't." Timmy exhaled, relieved that he had dodged the homophobic bullet. "Well, are there any other clowns like him?"

"Well, yes. There's one other gay clown, Bruce the Silly Goose and h—"

Timmy interrupted Silly Billy, "No, I mean are there any other Robot Clowns..."

"OHHH. Well, no, unless you count Steven from Michigan. He's such a bore ha ha! I tell ya if you invited Steven and some pigs over for dinner, the pigs would leave because of boredom. Ha ha, pigs! They love food!! Nah, we give Steven a hard time, but he's a good clown. It's just a bit of fun. But no... no, there are no other Robot Clowns."

Bing Bop approached the three clowns. Silly Billy gave Timmy a nudge and whispered, "Remember, just ignore him..."

"Wing Appleton, what's happening?" said Bing Bop as he started doing the robot.

"Oh nothing much Bing Bop! We're just chilling. What about you?" replied Klown.

"Klappity Eat, I'm enjoying this fun party we are having and dancing to the beat!"

"Ha ha right on, Bing Bop. You da clown!" laughed Klown.

"Uppity Po, I gotta go!" announced Bing Bop as he electronically walked away.

Timmy suddenly felt uncomfortable. Something about this encounter left him uneasy and he couldn't figure out what it was.

"I feel like he was trying to tell me something..." said Timmy. "I can't put my finger on what it is though..."

"Don't be silly, Timmy!" remarked Klown as he pulled Timmy over and bought another round of drinks.

20: That Might Take a Little More Than Paracetamol to Fix

Timmy woke up the next morning feeling the devil's notorious sauce all over his body. His first thought put the fear of god into him: *'training soon.'* Timmy's alarm clock was hidden under a watermelon. Nothing wrong with this, but that's how crazy of a night it was. *'What a wild night,'* Timmy thought. *'These clowns are going to be the death of me.'* The clock showed 8am which left Timmy in two minds:

1. Thank God training is in 2 hours, and

2. Oh snap! I only got half an hour of sleep.

He stood to his feet, wobbling in the process. A white noise was ringing in his ear. This was the first of many things to annoy him that morning. He held his nose shut with one hand and blew out as if he was trying to sneeze. **HONK.** The white noise went. It must have been the club music.

Timmy opened the window to recirculate the room with fresh air. Just as he was walking back to his bed, he heard familiar voices from outside, coming from three stories below. He gripped the outer ledge of the window to lean his chest and head outside of it. It was his coaching staff setting up cones for the drill that was due in 2 hours. Once again, Timmy tried to use his lip-reading abilities as the voices only sounded like murmurs from where he was standing.

"Let's go wake that little month up!" Timmy read from Jack's lips.

'It is the start of February after all, so that part makes sense, but what an odd way of phrasing it,' Timmy thought.

Desperate for sleep, he returned to bed right after setting his alarm for 9am. To his amazement the sleep didn't seem that long at all. Although, it wasn't his alarm clock that woke him. He rolled over as quick as a flick of the wrist to see Drump and Jack standing over him. He glanced in the mirror behind them, looked at himself with spread out arms and said, "Here we go again!"

Training was intense, backbreaking, and relentless. The combination of Drump and Jack working on Timmy was as if Coach Carter and Coach Boone came together to work on Timmy. The day started with unicycling, then continued with unicycling and then finished with unicycling. That's all there was to it. Like a wise clown named Wongo once said when he was competing years ago, "If you just keep unicycling non-stop, as fast as you can and ignore the pain, like, how couldn't you win?"

This quote from the multi-gold circuit winner has been written across gyms and training camps all over the Clownbound universe. Those words have also been known to inspire even Mother Teresa to cure ten more children. Those words gave her the energy to keep going when she simply thought she could not. Even though the words had nothing to do with curing sick children, she thought they did because she was very old. After hours of unicycling and multiple cramps, the final day of training was over. It looked as though it was paying off because Timmy was in impeccable shape. That night he slept like a log. A log that'd had an incredibly tiring day, that is.

It was finally the night before the big race. The unicycling had been done and the mental preparation was in order. Suddenly, Drump busted into Timmy's room.

"Hey kid, you ready?!"

"Ready for sleep you mean?"

"Ha ha ha ha ha! What are you talking about? The big finale festival is on tonight. The night before the Olympics end," Drump said pulling in his stomach while buttoning up his plain white shirt.

"Do you not think I should be resting, coach?"

"Absolutely not! You're either going to win or you're not at this point. There's not a lot we can do from here that will enhance your odds of winning, until the big man fires the starter pistol."

"Gee whiz, are you sure, coach?"

"Of course I'm sure. I'm your coach, aren't I? Now put on some Paco Ruclown and start dressing dapper." Drump then left the room with the door still slightly open.

"But hey Timmy… I'm not your coach tonight am I? Ha ha. Let's get weird," said Drump slipping his head sideways through the crack in the door.

(Unfortunately, there is no 100% true story about this night. After every night out, the Clown Priests hold confession for all the bad men for being bold. Timmy arrived at the confession box early. There was a queue and Drump was at the top of the queue, while Jack was already in there. All the bad men had sore heads from the previous night, so you could hear a pin drop (Or a confession from the confession box). This is what Timmy heard.)

<u>Jack</u>

"Alas! Last night, night before the circuits! How could I forget! Sure, it was only a few hours ago. Me mateys and me made sail for the downstairs camp bar before setting course for the real party on the street. The crew were eager to unfold the night's treacherous tale, because we are bad buckos. But we wanted to get drunk fast, so we played a little game. I learned this game while I was voyaging the seven seas. On board we would be clenching a bottle of rum and whenever we spotted a whale, we would drink. It didn't take us too long to start feeling the waves of the drink hitting us, YARHAR! This tavern was full of whales. The bucko behind the counter ran out of drink before you could say 'Bob's your buccaneer'. So, we played that game until the sun went down and left the bar tipsy at best.

"After the bar, the night didn't last very long for me. Timmy and Drump wanted to head into some club to party down and maybe get some booty, but I was tired and ready for the fishes. Cause once any creature hits that mood, there's no coming back from it, is there? And I really hate to be a party pooper around me mateys. To save coin outside the club, Drump, very scoundrelly, had a litre of rum under his trendy bomber jacket. The scurvy bastard must have swiped it from the cabinet at the tavern we were at. Regretfully, I shared a few sips. I'm only partly human after all. I'm always naturally optimistic and try to get a buzz back if I can... There is no use even trying to chase that so-called buzz when bags are starting to form under your eyes. You're best off just to look after yourself and go back to your bunk. Which leads me to my final part of me tale.

"Drump was about to plunder from the rum...Then he got angry at me for nothing in the queue. I didn't wanna cause too much of a yo-ho-ho, so respectfully stepped out of line, to let that mad man calm down. Of course, I was angry, but I'd never hit one of me own in anger. Pirate code. I spotted with me nifty telescope three lovely looking lads tapping their thumbs on IBM Simons - what to me looked like compasses. I strolled up to them and began speaking French. The language of love. I'm a very well-travelled pirate, as you know. Bonjour les hommes! Which means 'a lovely night we're having.' They then replied, 'Fuck off back to the Caribbean you, pervert.' I thought they were just playing hard to get, so I dropped anchor and tried my arm again. 'Je peux vous offrir un verre?' which means 'I am really cool and really sexy also.' It sounds a lot better in French. They all glanced at me, rolled their eyes and looked back down at their compasses. More than likely looking for the quickest route out of this terribly awkward situation.

"Unlike me, I gave up and wandered home quietly by myself. T'was a short walk home, although it gave me a lot of time to think. Maybe I am going to be alone forever. Could love be made for everyone except me? All I wanted to do was get out of there, go back to my ship, and find my two men of the sea, Ben and Jerry. I then would usually sit down, feel sorry for myself, and shovel the sea men into me. I might not have a plunder of silver or much charm behind this ragged beard and scurvy teeth. I do have a heart worth its weight in gold, though. I have a tattoo of an 'X' over my heart on my chest…because that's where my real treasure is hidden."

<u>Drump</u>

"Oh yes, last night. Oh god, LAST night... It was the best night, ask anyone, they'll tell you the very same, the best night in history. With a lot of great people, yes, the greatest people you could ever party with. As far as I can remember, the start of the night consisted of me going into Timmy's room and letting him know that the party was about to start. I wouldn't go near Jack's hotel room because whenever I went to her door, I heard her crying from outside the room. She probably wanted to remain by herself. I love Jack with all my heart, God knows I do! Her personal life is her own and I'd prefer not to get mine tangled up in hers. From there I waited on the two of them to come down to the camp bar. I regret to say I was waiting around for longer than I expected. By the time Timmy came down I was already pretty tipsy from all of that Circus Sauvignon. I knew Timmy could smell it on my breath and thank God he had some willpower not to drink or he would be crucified in the race this morning.

"Timmy was fine. The trouble started when Jack came down those spiral stairs. She didn't even have the decency or class to wipe the powder from her nose. Jack also had this game she wanted to play, 'Who can sniff the most?' She lay down a mountain of white powder as if she was a guest on the show 'Martha Stewart Living'. She then rubbed her face into the mountain and sang old French songs. Timmy was kind of just cowering away from the situation and looking back... I don't blame him! The fight Jack and the barman had was one of the most vicious I'd seen in years, and I'm a successful professional clown boxing coach. Luckily, I was there to break it up, but to my dismay in the process I accidently fell into the mountain of snow Jack had made... But I don't think it had any real effect on me as I still felt completely in control of myself.

"After getting kicked out of the bar, we felt we had no choice but to try and find a club on the street. Naturally we chose the one with the biggest queue. Timmy was a rockstar at this point and we could get V.I.P anywhere. Unfortunately, at the biggest club in town, 'Fire', we couldn't get in because Timmy, God bless him, didn't want to be recognised. He didn't want to draw attention to himself. I had a backup plan. I had a litre bottle of vodka under my jacket to get a bit silly in the line. I took a swig of it and passed it to Jack. Jack drank it all so fast that I didn't have a chance to stop her. If that wasn't bad enough, she continued to smash the empty bottle over her head, causing a scene and getting herself kicked out of the queue. Timmy was absolutely mortified and wanted to go home, but being the great coach that I am, I urged him to push onward.

"At the door, the bouncers weren't too keen on letting us in. SAD! As usual, clubs only want funny girls and hot monkeys. We were just about to be turned away, when the owner of the bar came out and recognised Timmy! We were brought straight into the V.I.P area. SCORE! In there we were meeting all the big celebrities attending the Olympics. It was almost as high profile as Circus Wimbledon. There were the likes of Robert Clowny Jr., Snoop Hotdogg, and I'll never forget the moment I met my favourite celebrity of all, God. We were having so much fun... Until the fire started. Because of a little fire, everybody had to evacuate the building. Just for the record, I also saw Jack looking through her telescope into a huge mirror on the side wall of the club. I think the poor gal was trying to find herself. That stuff she was sniffing definitely wasn't Vicks anyways.

"Outside the club, the firefighters and police were there already. I tried to go back in when I realised God wasn't outside, but the police held me back. They started shouting at me, 'Who started the fire? How did this happen!?' I said back, referring to Timmy and myself 'We didn't start the fire, it was already burning since the world's been turning! Tell him Timmy!' Timmy continued, 'We didn't start the fire, no we didn't light it, but we tried to fight it.' with an extreme lack of enthusiasm. I liked that he played along to my song in such a stressful situation, though. It was funny at the time because that song had just been played in the club. Guess you would have had to have been there, Father. The policeman momentarily toe tapped to the groovy jam, but then got back to business and threw us aside to question more people. After that, Timmy and I went home. Oh yeah and actually I pulled a girl that night. Timmy wasn't there at the time so don't bother asking him and he wouldn't know her anyways she's from out of town. She was hot too."

<u>Timmy</u>

"I very strongly do not want to talk about last night. Looking at my coaching staff at all after what happened is one of the toughest things I've ever had to do. However, for the history books of the Circus Olympics, I will do what I must, for future athletes to have the best possible chance of performing better. If this story can inspire even one of those athletes, well that's a success story right there. If this night was a FRIENDS episode it'd be called 'The one where Timmy starts to develop night terrors.'

"It all began in my room. I had one earphone in my right ear listening to the Rocky soundtrack. I only had one in, so I could stay alert of any attacks against me. It's been happening a lot recently. Well the night really escalated from when Drump came into my room demanding I join him and Jack on a night out, when I really should have just been resting. I figured my coach knew best, though. How was I meant to know any better? But I vowed to myself that I wouldn't get intoxicated in any way whatsoever. I got dressed all nice and put on cologne because I'm a respectable figure around these parts.

"When I was ready, I went down to the bar, where I found Drump sitting on a stool by himself. He was already in a very bad way as early as 7pm. Because I wasn't drinking, all I could really do was observe the man. The bar was actually really cool, it was an honesty bar. Which means they put faith in the customers paying for their drinks without a bartender. He put away litres by the minute. Little did I know he was a very aggressive drunk. Within minutes he was trying to pick a fight with anyone! He glanced around the bar and tried to make eye contact with someone, just so he could shout at them, 'What the fuck are you looking at!?" I think he would have normally shouted at me but subconsciously he knew I must stay in prime condition. An inner coach instinct maybe. Things escalated when Jack came on the scene, though.

"Jack jumped from two stories to the ground from the top of the spiral staircase. Her eyes were completely bloodshot red, and her eyelids simply couldn't be seen because they were open so intensely. Her entire face was covered in white powder. We knew she was fond of it, but she really went all out last night. Her face looked as white as Jack Frost in the movie 'Jack Frost' where Jack Frost is a snowman. There were a few old men in there with us and they were practically hiding from us. We had to leave, or she would've wrecked the campus bar which would have meant us not getting our security deposit back.

"We arrived at a nightclub called 'Very Cold' where Drump was an embarrassment. Jack came out and joined us in the queue minutes later. She was even more embarrassing. Jack was twitching and literally snapping at people, biting in their faces like an angry, rabies-diseased dog. Drump wasn't as scary but he was as bad. I saw him go over to a circle of Clown College students before queuing, threatening to stab them. The students gave him an unopened litre bottle of vodka and loadsa money.

"The bouncers of the club noticed the commotion and came out to us. Drump tried to fight the men but it was no use. Although, as they were carrying us to the gutter, the club's owner recognised me and brought us in. He was a huge fan of my boxing. His only condition was that I get in a picture with him, which I was flattered by. Walking into the club, I glanced over to an alley where Jack was hugging and crying with a spray dog."

Priest: "A spray dog?"

"Yeah, a dog that's lost or doesn't have a home."

Priest: "You mean a stray dog."

"No, SPRAY dog S-P-R-A-Y."

Priest: "Why would they be called spray dogs?"

"Because when they get dirty, their hair starts to go all out of shape and wild. So, it's like they're wearing hairspray."

Priest: "…Right, go on with the story."

"So, we got into the club. Inside, Drump was going crazy around everybody. It was the same behaviour as outside but because we were in a club it was acceptable behaviour. They even brought both of us into the V.I.P section because the owner was hanging around up there. I chatted for a while with the owner, but I can't really recall most of it because the club was so loud, and his words blended in with the music. Drump was getting a lap dance from one of the owner's strippers. I couldn't hear it, but I saw from the corner of my eye that the stripper was crying and running away from Drump. I stared into the owner's eyes, so he wouldn't see what problems Drump had potentially caused behind his back. We locked eyes for a long time talking about boxing. Then the music shut off and everyone was evacuating the building. I had no idea what was going on, but I just left with the owner. I couldn't find Drump and in the moment I was most concerned for myself.

"Outside, everyone who had left the club crowded the street and were looking back at the huge flames inside the club. A woman screamed on the other side of the crowd, followed by many gasps. I couldn't see what was going on. I rustled though the crowd until I could get a glimpse of the commotion. Still behind a crowd of people, I saw something levitate into the air. It was Jack, our Jack, floating 10 feet in the air, morphing before my eyes. She was taking her time doing it too. The top of her body was still Jack. Instead of legs, however, she had four dog legs. 5 minutes went by, and she was a full German Shepard. Everyone started to pet her sending her tail wagging at 100mph. It was nice to see her happy for a change. Just as I was going to give her a little pet, she ran off chasing a car with the spray dog she was hugging earlier. Puppy love.

"I walked back to the club, however, as I was about 50 yards from it I was met by firefighters refusing me entrance. They said it had been evacuated, and Drump was safe, however, I still couldn't find him. The race was hours away. I needed my management team. I knew Jack was safe, but Drump? Not so much. My fear left when an explosion came from the club and Drump flew through a window from the second floor, being followed by a blaze of fire like an explosion had just happened. Suspiciously enough, he was holding a flamethrower when he landed. Even more suspiciously, he dropped it when he got up. Nobody could identify him as he was in the mix of the crowd and covered in ash from the fire. I ran over to him and then we just ran through the crowds, into our rooms and went to bed. Ready and fit for the big race today!"

Priest: "Confession has ended. Go on now yee bad men!" (We have no idea what they say after confession, because we are not BAD MEN!)

Prior to the confessions, Jack had restored to her regular pirate form. She and Drump then went straight back to bed for a power nap to be fresh to watch Timmy's big race. Timmy went straight to the circuits from confession to get a feel for the ground and to do his stretches. It was an hour until the race and, despite being out all night, he was feeling fresh. He could tell some of the other athletes were nervous, just wanting the race to be over and done with. Timmy had trained hard for this and he wanted to enjoy every moment that the Circus Olympics had to offer. He even went over to fans to sign autographs and get his photo taken. He was the people's champion from what he had already brought to the occasion.

There were five minutes to go and neither Jack nor Drump had arrived. Timmy had visions of the night before and could easily see how they mightn't make the event. At the same time, the build-up, the suspense... How could they miss it? However, the time had come.

"Athletes take your positions!" Timmy took his place at his number four position, a hot favourite to win. When the announcer called Timmy's name, he got the loudest applause from everyone in the crowd. Respect isn't given, it's earned, and God knows he'd earned theirs. He told him last night.

As Timmy waved to the crowd, he saw them. Jack and Drump were walking gingerly along the side-line of the track. Timmy got so excited. Now he was ready, now gold was in sight, now was his time.

"On your mark!"

Timmy never broke eye contact with his coaches. *'Their heads must be so sore!'* he thought.

"Get set!"

Although not as sore as they were in that moment when Diego appeared behind them with duel-wielded pistols and shot both of them in the back of the head.

The sound of Diego's guns made all the other unicyclists dash forward. Every single one of them disqualified. Timmy stayed on his mark, in a state of disbelief.

"DISQUALIFIED!" announced the announcer. "We have a winner, folks!"

Timmy - Champion of The Circus Olympics.

Clownbound

21: Holy Mackerel

<u>A Magician's Poem</u>

We don't associate with other acts,
we remain in seclusion.

Their weakness is the problem,
of which we are the solution.

And with the shake of a wand,
we trap them in a delusion.

Then we wait till they're sure,
till there's no more confusion.

Content with their surroundings,
content with their inclusion.

They've accepted their place,
in this real world/dream fusion.

Alas, T'was not real,
it was merely
an illusion.

Timmy, the new champion of the Circus Olympics, stood frozen at the starting line. He couldn't believe what he had just seen. Fear and shock filled his body as tears rolled down his cheeks.

"Come with me if you want the truth." A mysterious, robotic looking clown grabbed Timmy and pulled him aside.

He brought Timmy into a small training room located north of the circuit, before revealing himself.

"Bing Bop? What are you doing here? My friends... Oh Clown, my friends are dead." Timmy started crying.

"Timmy Tim Tim Thompson... This is not your reality. I tried to warn you, this is NOT your reality," said Bing Bop in a serious, robotic accent.

"Bing Bop, what are you saying? Why aren't you saying your weird quirks at the beginning of each sentence? What's going on?"

"Timmy, I'm a flaw in the illusion! You need to wake up! I'm not gay, they just said that because they knew that would keep you away from me. You need to get back to your reality. If you die in your own illusion, you die in real life. There's only one way of getting out. To get back you have to say the magic two words. Those words are Hol—"

Bing Bop was interrupted by several shotgun shells through his metallic skull. As he dropped to the floor, Timmy saw Diego standing in front of him, now carrying a shotgun.

"I'll kill every damn clown in the world if I have to. I will avenge my lizard and there's nothing you can do about it!" shouted Diego as he aimed the loaded gun at Timmy.

"Look Diego, I know you're upset! I understand! I know what it's like to lose someone. I've lost everything! I've lost my parents, the woman I love, my best friends and Wongo. I've lost it all! Revenge isn't the answer!" pleaded Timmy.

It was useless. Diego aimed the gun at Timmy's chest and pulled the trigger. Timmy fell to the ground, pain aching through his body. He put his hands to his chest and saw the blood pour through his fingers.

He let out a roar, "Holy Mackerel!"

With that, he started to feel lightheaded, his vision started to go blurry. He looked around him as everything began to fade into a light grey colour. He felt himself rise above his body, looking down on himself and his surroundings. He was terrified. He felt like he had accidently smoked DMT with Joe Rogan. Suddenly, he lost consciousness.

Timmy woke up in a small room surrounded by three white walls and a glass opening, with a door clearly sealed shut. Behind the glass stood what appeared to be a security guard. He was pale white, with blonde cornrows and was listening to something on his Walkman. There were two other men in the room, one Hispanic man around Timmy's age and another much older, wise looking man with white hair and a long white beard. Timmy looked down and noticed his shoes were no longer on. In fact, his whole clown outfit wasn't on. He was now wearing some plain white t-shirt and grey sweatpants. He put his hands on his face momentarily, removing them and looking at them. No clown makeup. He was too confused to speak, frozen on the spot staring at his hands.

"You must have been out for weeks, kid. We assumed you were dead."

"What? Where am I? What's going on?" asked Timmy who was as confused as a dog in a nightclub.

"It's a long story... What's your name, kid?" asked the wise old man.

"T-Timmy. I was about to start the big circuit race..." Timmy took a deep shaky breath. "...and then I don't know what happened. Everything got weird... And then I woke up here. What is this place?"

The Hispanic man stood up. "This? This is hell!" he joked as he handed Timmy a pair of sunglasses. "Take these. It can be bright in here at the beginning. By the way, the name's Miguel."

"Wait. What date is it?" asked Timmy, as he put on the shades.

"We don't know... They don't let us have calendars believe it or not."

"Who's they?" asked Timmy who was starting to calm down like a dog who had just left a nightclub.

"You really don't remember? The Magicians, Timmy. They threw you and your friend in here about... what must have been a month ago. You were in full illusion," said the wise old man as he looked at Timmy with a sympathetic look.

"My friend?"

"Drump... It was the mighty Clown King Drump. He was conscious unlike you. He kept shouting at you to wake up, but you were as stiff as a stuffed dog."

"Drump's here? Where is he? He'll be able to explain what's going on!" said Timmy with a tone of enthusiasm.

The two men looked at each other before lowering their eyes towards the ground. The wise old man sighed, "Drump is gone..."

"Gone where? What do you mean?" pestered Timmy.

"They- he's dead, Timmy. I'm sorry. He's gone, but, funnily enough, his body has yet to be recovered."

"What? Oh no, please tell me you're lying. The last thing I can remember is seeing Drump and Jack walking towards the circuit race..." said Timmy, who was still struggling to recall what had happened.

"This can't be happening!" Timmy started shaking his head. "This is a dream or something. There's no way this is actually happening. I was LITERALLY JUST AT THE FINAL CIRCUIT RACE!" Timmy started shaking and having a minor panic attack.

Miguel put his hand on Timmy's shoulder, "Look Timmy, don't be mad at yourself. Very few people can withstand the Magician's illusions. We sure couldn't."

"No, but I did! I got away from them. They tried to trick me with the love of my life, Hybrid, but they said she liked trapezing which I knew wasn't true and we escaped!"

"I'm sorry, Timmy, but that's part of their illusion. They make it seem like you've beaten them. They want you to think that you're in control. Sometimes they'll have you in the illusion for years. Everything after that point was part of their illusion." The wise old man said as he stood up and approached Timmy.

"This can't be happening. It felt so real. So, everybody I've met over the past month aren't real? They're figments of my imagination?" Timmy said with defeat.

"Not quite," said the wise old man. "The Magicians can only create an illusion with those that are real. All of those people you met on your journey are real clowns, with real lives. Your relationships with them were real, but only to you. They may dream of you, but they will never know who you are or why they are dreaming of you."

Tears rolled down Timmy's cheeks as he tried to come to grips with this reality.

"Those bastards! They're going to win the Circus Olympics now!" he cried.

"The Circus Olympics!" laughed the wise old man, "This goes much deeper than the Circus Olympics, Timmy. The magicians wouldn't risk killing the mighty Drump over just another Circus Olympics. This is about the Crystals!"

"The what?" asked Timmy in complete confusion.

"The Circus Crystals, Timmy! Don't you know? The ten Circus Crystals! The objects holding together the very fabric of our reality!" The wise old man seemed genuinely surprised about Timmy's ignorance on the subject.

"Sorry, but I have absolutely no idea what you're talking about," admitted Timmy.

"Okay… okay, Timmy. I'll explain it to you now," said the wise old man.

"Uh oh, here he goes rambling again..." sighed Miguel from the other side of the room.

"You might want to sit down for this," the wise old man said to Timmy, who was already sitting down. "You see, Timmy, about two million years ago, when humans first evolved, the world was a very different place. That doesn't have anything to do with the crystals but isn't that crazy? Two million years! So anyway, skip forward to about 800BC and those Greek guys. The story says that one day Ancient Greece was struck by a meteorite, destroying half of all their population. Within the meteor were 10 small glowing rocks; perfectly round and all a different colour. The Greek oligarchy didn't know what to do so they called in the only people powerful enough to resolve the situation; the Circus. The Circus Research Centre spent hundreds of years analysing and studying these objects. As the years went on, they discovered that there was something strange about these crystals… they possessed some sort of power. Something they had never seen before. As soon as the Greeks heard about this they demanded access to the crystals. Knowing that the Greeks would abuse the crystals, the Circus had no choice but to destroy Greece."

Timmy started scratching his head in disbelief. "That's… kind of unbelievable… Even if that's true, which it's not, what does this have to do with us being here? What does this have to do with me?"

"Well, Timmy, I was getting to that before you interrupted me, wasn't I?" said the wise old man in a rather agitated tone.

"Once Greece collapsed, the crystals were split between the ten main factions of the Circus to hide and protect. This is what World War 1 and a half was REALLY about. Every once in a while someone so evil and so craving of chaos comes along and attempts to gather all the crystals and that is what is happening right now, Timmy! And, because of this, the Magicians now possess 6 of the Crystals: the Magician Crystal, the Tightrope Walker's Crystal, the Contortionist's Crystal, the Acrobat's Crystal, the Trapeze Artist's Crystal and now the Clown Crystal."

"The Clown Crystal?" said Timmy in shock. "How did they get the Clown Crystal?"

The wise old man shook his head in disappointment. "You, Timmy, you! I don't know who gave you the ring, Timmy, but whoever did obviously trusted you more than they should have."

"Drump gave it to me… I had only met him that day and he handed me the ring. I didn't know it had any true value. Why would he give it to me?"

"Perhaps he saw something in you… or maybe he was drunk. I don't know. Either way we're in big trouble now!"

"B-but they can't do anything until they have 10 Crystals right?" pleaded Timmy.

"I wish that were how it worked! As I said, they become more powerful with each Crystal. Up until the fifth Crystal all of their abilities were miniscule but the ability they will now possess is truly terrifying. We must hope and pray that they do not get all 10 Circus Crystals, because at that point there will be no going back."

"What ability? What can do they do now?" asked Timmy.

"They can... r-raise..." The wise old man took a deep breath. "Raise the dead. They can raise the dead and have them fight for them."

Clownbound

"Oh good Clown!" gasped Timmy, just about holding his sick down. "Where are the remaining Crystals?"

"9 of them are on Earth, and the tenth is on Primatomorphia, or as we like to call it, the Planet of the Primates."

"If we want to save the world, we will need your help, Timmy!"

"I can't do anything. I don't have my clown costume, my makeup or even my clown props. I won't stand a chance," said Timmy with a defeated sigh.

"Have you learned nothing?" The wise old man stood up and squared up to Timmy. "Is that what you think we are, Timmy? Do you think we're a bunch of guys dressing up in silly costumes, putting on ridiculous makeup and using stupid props to impress children? Is that what you think we are!? Clearly you haven't been paying attention. Being a clown is not about what we wear! It's not about whether we wear makeup or not! It's about our mindset! It's not a job, Timmy, Goddammit! This is not a hobby! This is a blessing, a gift! When a child is dying of thirst and a man hands them a bottle of water, that's a clown! When a woman is stuck down a well, and you hand them a rope, that's being a clown! Being a clown is helping those that need help and the whole damn planet needs our help, Timmy. You don't need that costume, you don't need that makeup and you sure as hell don't need those props, Timmy! You don't need them! This is what you need!" The wise old man pointed at Timmy's heart, "The Magician's power is their ability to create illusions. Have you never wondered what our power is, Timmy? Our superpower is love! Love for one another, love for all. We are the people who rise to the occasion and protect the world, even when we know they wouldn't do the same for us. People have been laughing at clowns for centuries, Timmy, and that's just fine.

We've incorporated that into our acts now, but we can't forget our true purpose. To protect the people from themselves."

"God dammit, you're right! We have to help! We have to get out of here and stop them before it's too late!" demanded Timmy.

Miguel chuckled, "If we could get out of here, don't you think we would have done it by now, my mans?"

"Wait," said the wise old man as something clicked in his head, "there is one way. I kept it quiet because it's a two-man job and I'm too old. But the two of you could."

Timmy and Miguel looked at each other with an expression of hope. The two men gathered around the wise old man to hear his plan.

"It won't be easy. But at two o'clock every day I've noticed the Magician Guards switch duty. While they swap, there's a 5-minute gap which you will need to use, and you'll need every second of it. There's a vent at the top right corner of this cell. One of you will need to climb through it and get to the opposite side of the cell. Once there, you can open the door by turning the handle. There's a safety lock on this side. Unfortunately, there's a second door. To open the second door, we'll need to have all the circuitry shut off for at least two minutes. That's a two-man job. Both of you will have to get through to the circuits and shut them off. Miguel should know how to get there."

"Ayyy you know it boy," responded Miguel.

"Okay. Once that's done, you're out. It really is that simple. But we MUST do it right the first time. Otherwise, they'll heighten the security and we'll never get another chance. Which one of you will climb through the vent?"

"I'll do it!" exclaimed Timmy. "What time is it now?"

The wise old man looked at his bare wrist before sarcastically remarking, "Let me just check the watch they let us keep..."

"Well that's great," said Timmy in what could also be considered a sarcastic tone. "So how will we know when its two o'clock?"

"Oh, we'll know," replied the wise old man with a nod.

After ten minutes of jail cell banter between the three men, Timmy knew exactly what the wise old man meant when he said they'll know. The security guard looked at his watch and said, "Huh! 2 O'clock already... Huh! How's about that!"

The wise old man turned to Timmy. "He says the exact same thing every day. That's the signal... Go!"

With that, Timmy threw himself through the vent in cinematic fashion. Landing spectacularly on the other side, he adjusted his shades and headed for the cell. Looking at the wise old man and Miguel, he had to get the door open. He turned the handle. No luck; the door remained shut. Sweat was pouring down his face. What was he to do? In a moment of incredible intuition, he looked at the key in the keyhole below the handle. *What if I turn this and then try again* thought Timmy as he turned the key. Holding his breath, he turned the handle for the second time. Success. The door opened. The three men let out a sigh of relief.

"Genius thinking on the spot!" roared the wise old man.

"Thank you! Now, Miguel, I'm going to need you to..." Timmy took off his shades and turned his head towards Miguel.

"What is it, Timmy? What do you ask of me? I'll do it! Anything! Just get me out of this damn cell!" shouted Miguel, with sweat pumping down his forehead.

"Huh! What do I want? I want you to... Take me to the circuits."

FIN

To be continued…?

Clownbound
Acknowledgments:
Seán Dalton

I have absolutely no idea how to write an acknowledgement, so I'm going to structure this around what I'm reading online. To my wife. I don't have a wife. To my family. I do have a family. And I will thank them now.

A VERY important thanks to **my mother**. Thank you for being unbiased and honest, and for letting me run jokes (some really awful jokes) by you almost every day.

I'd like to thank **my dad** and my step-mother, **Sinead**. I know I didn't tell either of you about the book until it was written, but from that point on, you two have been nothing but supportive and helpful.

I'd like to thank my brother, **Ryan** and my sister, **Teagan**. Thanks, Ryan, for giving us the idea for the cover and listening to me talk about Clownbound for months on end.

Moving on from immediate family, I'd like to thank **all the lads.** Ha Ha Yes!! The Lads!!!
Especially, **Chipper Dave**; our editor, our confidant, our… editor. This book would be far worse than it already is without your involvement.

I'd like to thank those who read early drafts of the book; **Conor Kelly, Jack Cummins, Orla Carroll.** Conor, you saying, "It's fixable," was genuinely a moment that made me think, *'Maybe it's fixable.'* Jack, you helped us add more to the story, as well as some other things (wink wink). Orla, you helped greatly on the last hurdle with the editing and the general story.

And the biggest thanks goes to **Seán Kelly** for asking me to write this novel with him in the first place. I definitely wouldn't have been able to write this by myself (because it was your idea).

Seán Kelly

As co-author and visionary of the Clownbound Universe I want to thank Seán Dalton for coming on this adventure with me. Mad to think that we didn't have a book at one point, isn't it? Huh? Me you? Book? Yeah? Gas, isn't it! HAHA the lads! YES!

I would like to thank my brother David Kelly for being very supportive and patient for the book to come out.

And to my girlfriend, Muffins, u up? And if you are, wua?

End Credits

(Just imagine they're rolling. Cover with your hand as you move down if needs be.)

Seán Kelly ------------------------------ Co-author

Seán Dalton ----------------------------- Co-author

David O'Rourke -------- Editor and First Reader

Conor Kelly -------------------------- First Reader

Ryan Dalton --------------------------Early Reader

Janette O'Neill --------------------Listener of Ideas

Ciaran Hegarty ------ Driver of the lads to work

Jack Cummins -----------------------Early Reader

Orla Carroll ----------------------- Early Reader

Clownbound

Paddy Dalton --------------------------Early Reader

Michael Kelly -----Owner of house Sean lives in

Ruby Towers -------------------------------Legend